Shadows
of
Humiliation

Deborah Carter

ISBN 978-0-473-74320-8
ISBN 978-0-473-74321-5
ISBN 978-0-473-74322-2
ISBN 978-0-473-74323-9

<u>**Dedicated to**</u>

To my library dwellers for keeping me motivated.

Chapter One

"Whoa boy," a voice rang out, and the shuddering boards beneath Abigail's feet stilled, although the carriage continued to sway a moment or two longer, the momentum slowly becoming less and less until it finally ceased.

She was hopeful; quietly optimistic that they hadn't yet reached their destination, for she'd prayed this journey would never reach its end. Now, she pleaded with the very universe itself that this was to be another stop, just another night at an Inn to feed and rest the horses and their driver.

When she'd first been instructed that she was to travel South, West to meet Mr Langley, the man her father had promised her too, she had been overwhelmed, a little fearful but also excited, this could be an adventure, she was going away. She'd expected a day's train journey; her first time on the steam locomotive, and she had been eager for the experience, only to have her excitement dashed when the carriage had shown at the door. Within those four long, lonely days shut in the swaying carriage, the thrill for adventure had quickly dissipated, and her fear of the unknown had set her nerves on edge. And now, all she wanted was for another four days, and another, never to reach the destination and the man she was to wed. Sadly, what she wanted was not to be; she'd arrived.

All was quiet, save the snorting of the horses and the jingle jangle of the harness as the great animals shuffled their hooves, searching to find a more comfortable footing amongst the stones along the carriageway. Wood creaked as the driver climbed from his bench and his footfalls scuffed and echoed in the cold, misty air that enveloped her conveyance. Each footstep brought her closer to her impending doom. The door beside her swung back, and the short man in his dark, thick overcoat, damp with tiny droplets of mist, manoeuvred a step for her to dismount from the safe place she'd been clinging to for the last three days.

"Miss?" he mumbled, offering her his hand.

Abigail didn't know this driver; he'd pulled up to her father's home mere days ago. He'd been a stranger who had looked after her during this unnerving journey, and now as she took his proffered fingers, she found herself unwilling to let go, wishing he would close the door, climb back onto his bench and drive on and on.

Standing awkwardly, her neck bent so as not to strike her head on the low roof, Abigail stepped shakily onto the waiting step and then to the cold, hard stones.

The helping hand disappeared as the driver moved away and began to unload her luggage from the holding shelf at the rear of the carriage, he muttered to himself as he tugged the hardened leather straps from the dull silver buckles, huffing as he lifted and groaned as he bent, gently placing the chest of belongings on the leaf-strewn driveway.

Soothing down the grim, grey coat her mother had chosen for her to wear, which covered an even grimmer, darker grey gown chosen for her new role as mistress of this house; She attempted to get her shaking hands and nerves under control. Glancing to the heavens for a moment to gather her thoughts and courage, she was interrupted when the large front door swung open, and she was engulfed in a slender shaft of light. She took a deep breath and bent her knees, lifting the smaller bag and turned to thank the driver, whose shrewd eyes stared through heavy brows as he lit a small pipe, the tiny flame showing her his look of uncertainty.

Turning away, she took in the dark, looming building, noting how it dwarfed the tiny archway of light that seemed to beckon; deep down she knew, one step inside and she would be lost, swallowed whole. Courage deserted her, legs weak and body shaking, she stood like a statue.

"Damn it, woman. Get inside before you catch your death." His voice came to her, loud in the gloomy darkness. Bowing her head in resignation she began the final part of her journey, she trudged reluctantly toward the dark silhouette which near filled the door frame. Mr Langley was intimidating, not just his loud, angry voice, but every aspect of him. His build, tall and muscular, unlike the gentlemen, acquaintances, business colleagues who visited her father's estate, who all appeared short and pale, with soft hands and paunchy middles.

Abigail reached the door and stood waiting for him to stand aside, and when he didn't budge, she finally looked up, and up into his shadow filled features. She'd only seen this man once before, when she'd peeked through the stair railings safe in her father's home, and the imposing giant of a man had frightened her as he stood in the small drawing room. She'd shrunk back away out of sight when he'd turned in her direction, positive that he hadn't seen her, but then saw her father's head move and he too stared intently at the spot where she had crouched. Now, here in his own domain, frightening wasn't the word she'd use, no, if she could find her voice, the word 'terrifying' would be what passed her lips.

He made her feel small, when in all reality, she herself was a decent height for a lady; Mr Langley however, dwarfed her slender body with his thick, muscular frame, his wide shoulders dominating the too small space. His whiskered chin was squared, not unappealing, but a little hard, intimidating. His lips, although in an angry line right now, looked soft, tilting slightly at the edges as if used to being in a smile and not a scowl. Two deep-set eyes, dark and shadowed by the frown marring his forehead, regarded her as he looked down his nose and her eyes quickly shied to the left, coming to rest on the long-jagged scar, the skin an unusual iridescent pinkish-white and slightly raised, it journeyed from just below his right eye, curved down over the high cheekbone and stopped just above his lip. He didn't allow her perusal for long as he turned the other cheek to her and raised his arm indicating for her to move.

"Come in, Miss Dumont," he said as his body turned side-on to allow a small passage for her to gain access into the house. She moved slowly, eyes down, staring at the hard wooden floor as she hugged the wall as close as possible so as not to make contact with the giant beside her. She jumped as the door closed with a loud boom.

"My things, Sir, they are still in the drive." Abigail whispered.

"Jackson will bring them up once he's stabled the horses," he replied and waved her forward towards another door. "Move yourself woman, you'll not warm yourself standing in the entry way."

Shuffling forward toward the door he indicated, she twisted the knob and gave the wood a slight nudge and stepped into a much larger room with Mr Langley nipping at her heels. He tugged the door from her numb fingers, and she winced as he pushed the wood back into place with a decisive click and leaned his back against it, effectively locking her in. The sight of the large open fireplace with flames licking the logs stacked in the grate should have been a welcome sight, but with the door closed, the sudden heat was overwhelming on her cold skin. Her cheeks reddened, as her blood warmed, thawing her shivering body and stiff fingers, the prickling heat making her want to scratch, but she willed her hands to be still.

"Sit!" the command made her start, and the small bag dropped from her fingers as her hands flew to clutch at her chest, her heart pounding rapidly within. "For the love of …" he moved away from the door and leaning down, drew her belongings up and delivered them on the long table with a toss of his wrist. "Miss Dumont, please remove your coat and take a seat, warm yourself before I show you to your room.   It is late! I won't be needing anything from you tonight," with another wave of his hand he indicated one of the two seats in front of the fire, and Abigail moved woodenly forward, slowly dragging the coat from her arms. Without it, she felt like she'd lost a pierce of her armour, and the shivering began again in earnest. Draping the coat over the back of the chair she sank onto the cushion, back stiff and fingers twisting nervously in the material of her gown. Her eyes cast toward the flickering flames, concentrating on calming her pounding heart, and thus not seeing Mr Langley's movements; her body flinched in surprise as he pushed a glass into her hand. "Drink," he ordered, and she did, taking a gulp of the amber liquid before coughing and spluttering as the heat took her breath, it burned a line of fire down her throat and pooled like a lava pit in her chest; she'd never tasted anything like it. "More," he insisted helping her tilt the glass to her lips, as she eyed him over the rim, tears shimmering, but complied to his command. The second shot, if anything, burned hotter than the first, and she would have coughed if the man had given her a chance to do so before tipping the glass a third time and she had no choice but to take another gulp of the searing fluid. "There, that should do it," he muttered and withdrew the glass from her fingers, pouring the small amount left into his own glass and emptying it in one graceful shot, and then poured himself another and took a seat in the chair opposite her. He nursed the drink in his hand as his eyes studiously swept upward, taking in the dowdy gown and her stiff posture before stopping at her face and capturing her gaze. "Hungry?" he queried.

Abigail shook her head; she hadn't eaten since breakfast, but with the fiery alcohol burning, and the nervous churning in her gut, she couldn't have eaten without embarrassing herself, knowing the food would surely make a second appearance.

She sat in silence, cheeks burning as she felt the man's scrutiny and was thankful for the heat of the crackling fire which must surely hide the embarrassing flush. Curious as Abigail was, she couldn't bring herself to gaze around the room in case she encountered those eyes, so she continued to watch the flames, mesmerised by how they licked and caressed the logs, before consuming them.

She wondered if her luggage had been brought in or was still gathering moisture out on the stones. Almost as if the man opposite had read her thoughts, he said, "Jackson will deliver your belongings to your room, I'll show you through shortly after a quick perusal of the kitchen. Jackson requires breakfast for 6 a.m., I'll be taking mine a half hour later." Throwing his head back, he drained his glass and stood, placing the empty tumbler on a small table she hadn't noticed beside his chair, which held a book and a box of cigars.

Following his lead and standing, she cleared her still burning throat to ask, "And what of me, Mr Langley, do you expect my company, am I to be up at the crack of dawn also?" She inwardly cringed at the very idea of leaving her bed before the sun had risen. Why, the only time she'd ever done so back home was four days prior, when she'd been told an early start was advantageous to the travel plans, assuring they arrived at their nightly accommodations before darkness set in. Travelling at night was far too dangerous with the highwaymen which roamed the roads, ambushing, robbing and murdering unlucky travellers.

"I don't dine with the servants, Miss Dumont! You shall partake of your meal after you've attended me; mine will be served here in the dining room," he indicated the large table behind where they were seated, "there is a table and chairs in the kitchen for yourself and Jackson. Now, if you are quite warm enough, I'll show you the kitche …"

"Servant!" her outraged voice interrupted him. She coughed past the burn in her throat, "How dare you, Sir. I am no servant, and I shan't be rising at the crack of dawn to attend the likes of you."

Mr Langley stared down at her, his bushy eyebrows dipping into a frown and nearly covering the forest green of his eyes, his fierce gaze capturing hers. "You may not have been a servant, Miss Dumont, but I require exactly that of you. Why would you be here other than to work in my kitchen?"

"I... I," she stuttered as her thoughts flew back to the heated conversation she'd held with her father.

"Abigail, do as Mr Langley tells you and you'll soon have him eating out of your hand. The gentleman couldn't have chosen a more perfect specimen, a lady of class and breeding, someone reliable to oversee the running of his home whilst he's away on business, as your dear mama does. And then for him to come home to a beautiful, dutiful wife, why, what more could a man want?" Her argument that she didn't know this man, had never heard of him, and wondered how he knew of her, fell on deaf ears, but her father had made the match and as his daughter, she would comply to his expectations. Except now, the prickling heat clawing its way up her neck, and the heavy feeling in her gut was telling her that maybe, just maybe her father had made a grave error in his judgement.

"I...I, I mean we, we are to be wed so I can manage your household for you whilst you are away. M-my father said when you visited, it was myself whom you requested to undertake the journey to your home."

His unexpected guffaw shocked her, his loud laughter filling the room and Abigail's head began to swim alarmingly, so much so that she took a swaying step back, her boots knocking against the blackened stones of the fire surround and she overbalanced, knocking and felling the chair in which she'd sat. The hearth appeared to rise to meet her, and she could feel the heat on her face, panic surged, and her arms flew out searching for something, anything to stop her descent but they merely knocked at the blackened bricks, there was nothing to grasp. She closed her eyes waiting for the inevitable; for the flames to sear her skin.

One moment she was falling and then with a jolt, she hovered, toes barely touching the floor as a steel band wrapped around her torso holding her motionless for one heartbeat, two, and then she was swung, up off the floor, and another steel band hooked beneath her knees. She felt like she was floating as he carried her, pressed into his hard chest, across the room, settling her gently onto a hard wooden surface and the iron bands disappeared.

The smell of singeing material invaded her nostrils and glancing at Mr Langley to see if he too had smelt it, was shocked by the sudden whirr of movement as he began batting and dragging at her gown; she was dragging herself away from him when a searing pain burst along her calf, and she realized he was not trying to hurt her, he was trying to save her, she was on fire. A loud RRRIP sounded as he tore at the burning material, and chilled air touched her knees, but she was not looking for any damage. No, her eyes were drawn to the man towering above her, holding the torn, smoking material in his fist. Her eyelids fluttered, she blinked once, twice and then darkness pulled her into its sweet embrace.

Chapter Two

Edward Langley gazed at the unconscious woman atop his dining table. He held in his fist the blackened material which he'd literally torn from her body; he'd managed to slap the ignited embers away, but not before they'd scorched the skin across Miss Dumont's inner calf. A whisp of smoke caught his attention and he quickly moved to stamp out the burning ember on the dark rug that lay before the hearth and pulled the chair and Miss Dumont's coat, well away from where the hungry flames had been reaching toward the wooden furniture. The heat from the flame already enough to cause the oils which coated the dark wood, to bubble and blister. He paid it no mind; the wood would be easy to rub down and the lacquer reapplied. The cushion however had not fared so well and was burning brightly on the hearth, and he used the toe of his boot to manoeuvre it further into the grate, throwing the fistful of material he held alongside it and watched as it smoked and burst to flame, before turning back to check on the troublesome female on his table.

The reddened skin on her leg demanded his attention, even as his fingers itched to caress the soft, satiny flesh showing just above her stocking. He clenched his fists, resisting the temptation to touch, and turned his gaze to her injured calf, where wicked red blotches marred the alabaster skin; the wound would undoubtedly blister, and he knew he needed to cool the burn. Moving with long strides down the hall to the kitchen, he collected a clean cloth from the neatly folded bundle in the cabinet, placed a bowl in the sink, and spun the tap, cold water gushed, and he half-filled the bowl.

Seizing a couple of clean towels, he headed back to the dining room and placing the bowl on the table beside Miss Dumont, he eyed her motionless form. Undressing a woman was something he'd done numerous times, but he'd never drawn down the stocking of an unconscious lady. He sighed as his fingertips caressed the silken strip of her garter, shook his head and concentrated on the task at hand. Peeling what was left of the sheer stocking down her leg; he removed her shoe and rolled the stocking over her heel, tugged it until it slipped from her toes and then dropped it to the floor.

He dipped the cloth into the cold water and placed it against the angry red flesh. Dipped it again twice more before draping the cloth, being sure to cover the entirety of the burn. He realized the dripping cloth was soaking her gown, he snatched up the dry towels, shaking out the creases then rolled them lengthwise, a towelling sausage, which he tucked carefully down the outside of the woman's leg. The other was riskier, knowing if she woke whilst fitting the towel between her legs, there would be hell to pay. Trying his hardest to stop his hands from following his thoughts, envisioning them running up the remaining flimsy stocking, up over the garter to the silky skin of her uninjured thigh. He bit down on a groan and pushed the other roll in the small space where her legs slightly parted in hopes they would absorb the excess water. Once done, he refilled his glass and pulled his chair in close to the table, every so often dribbling more cold water onto the cloth, keeping cool the heated skin beneath.

He studied her as he sipped his whiskey and wondered how the hell, he'd managed to get himself into this mess. He knew he probably shouldn't have laughed at her proclamation of intended marriage; it was probably a little rude, but he couldn't help it. How had she ever reached such a conclusion? She had after all, only weeks ago, turned her back on his cousin. Refusing to see him, speak with him. And what game was her father playing, had he decided the rumours were true and had a change of mind? Had he been searching for the next man to hoist his daughter on? Edward took another mouthful of his whiskey, swirling it around his mouth for a moment before letting the heat slide from his tongue and swallowing. His eyes played over her face. She was a beauty! His cousin, Spencer had described her as being very pretty, with long, red hair and the eyes of a witch; green tunnels which entranced and entrapped. But Spencer's description had been sadly lacking. Her hair was not red, but a deep auburn and as to its length, Edward couldn't determine as Miss Dumont had captured the thick tresses in a tight bundle at the back of her head. Her eyes, when she had glowered at him were like green turbulent waters, with tiny, swimming gold flecks.

He let his gaze wander further taking in the dreadful grey gown, ruined now by the fire and by his hand. But as ugly as the garment was, it was unable to undermine the slender column of her neck, the slight width of her shoulders and a firm bosom which had heaved a little in her anger. Nor did it hide her tiny pinched-in waist; Why, when he'd caught her during her fall, his arm had banded right around her slim frame. His eyes traversed further, stopping at the creamy white flesh of her uninjured leg, how soft would her skin be? With a mind of their own, his fingers reached out, the tips barely teasing the cool, silken skin as he trailed them a little higher, his breathing quickened, and jealousy aimed at

Spencer heated in his veins, that his cousin had delighted in her tantalizing flesh.

The woman bolted upright, and Edward hissed in a breath and snatched his fingers from her leg and tilting his head, locked eyes with a pair of angry green orbs.

"Mr Langley!" her bosom heaved, and his eyes flicked down as if hypnotised, before dragging them back up to her face. Pushing his chair back, he stood quickly, realizing that seated beside the table as he had been, suddenly seemed wrong as if he'd laid a meal out before himself and was sat down to feast. He inhaled sharply at his thoughts, yes indeed, he would very much like to feast on Miss Dumont using his mouth, his tongue, and his teeth to bite down and mark that alabaster skin; he shook the visual from his mind and took a big step back, before he decided 'to hell with it', and acted out his fantasy.

Needing to take back control, his words came out sharp, defensive. "Miss Dumont, when I ask in future if you are hungry, I expect the truth. You fainted dead away! When did you last eat?" Her eyes grew wider if that was possible, and she turned away looking down the length of the table where she regarded his handywork, the bowl, her ripped garment and the risqué placement of the towel between her legs. Her face flushed pink, the embarrassment of her predicament making her snap back.

"Really? Mr Langley. You wish to question my dietary intake instead of explaining why my gown is shredded and why your hand was on my person?"

"I feel my question was perfect for the predicament in which you find yourself, Miss Dumont. If you had eaten when I suggested, you wouldn't have become lightheaded when you stood, thus you wouldn't have fallen and set my dining room on fire and your gown with it. I merely removed the burning part of the garment, although not before it seared your leg. I was, when you came round, applying a cooling aid to reduce the heat to your injury," he lied.

"Oh," she breathed, and the fight left her, only to be replaced by mortification when she realized she was laid on the dining table, the towel parting her legs, and said legs laid bare to his gaze. Leaning forward she grasped the ragged edges of material, dragging it across her uninjured leg and heard him inhale, a deep breath but she wouldn't, couldn't look at him. "Sir, if you'd be so kind as to assist me from the table," her voice shook slightly and she withdrew the damp towel from between her legs, draping it over the knee of her injured leg then swung herself around, effectively giving him her back.

Edward smiled to himself and moved around the furniture to aid her as she asked. She held her hand out to him, which he ignored, and thrusting one strong arm beneath her knees and the other rounding her back, he lifted her bodily from the table and walked with her across the room, seating her on the chair where he'd previously sat. "Stay there," he ordered and left the room, returning to the kitchen he retrieved a muslin wrapped loaf from the box, butter and ham slices from the plate in the larder, then carried them all back through to the dining room and deposited the ingredients on the clear end of the table. Quickly slicing through the loaf, he slathered on butter and slapped a thick wedge of ham down, added a second piece of bread, and walked over to her. "Eat," he thrust the doughy meal into her hands and walked back to the sideboard to pour himself another whiskey. He stood, leaning against the wall, one knee bent, drinking whilst watching her nibble at her food and realised frustratedly that he would have to break the awkward silence.

"My apologies for startling you, Miss Dumont. However, your somewhat pretentious comment was most laughable. I could not help myself. I am however aggrieved that you were injured because of it. I suggest you tell me exactly what information your father shared with you, so we may both know where we stand."

Edward watched her face pale, and she replaced the piece of bread she'd been nibbling, back onto the plate. She swallowed with difficulty, and he moved quickly, offering her his glass, which she accepted with a shaking hand, and took a deep sip, nodding her thanks, but instead of returning it, she kept it clutched between her hands; if she was to speak the words her father had said, she felt she may need more of the mind -numbing liquid.

"M-my father," she started, then took a deep breath and steadied her voice, "shared that you wished for me to travel to your estate, although how you had even heard of me, I cannot fathom," she added. "To keep house and manage your home whilst you were away on your business endeavours as a wife should." She finally raised her head, her eyes warily finding the grim look on his face, and the anger flashing in his eyes.

"You cannot fathom whence I heard of you?" he drawled. "You are not unknown in town Miss Dumont, dances and parties. I admit, I rarely visit town these days and therefore had not the pleasure of an introduction to you or your family personally, that was until I was introduced to your father at a gambling house."

"What? No, you must be mistaken, Sir. My father doesn't gamble." Her father at a gaming table? No! He had a great dislike of gambling, or so she had been led to believe. Why, he rarely accepted the social invitations sent to the house, which meant Mama and the family had missed many of the gay affairs in which others of their standing enjoyed.

Admittedly he would occasionally venture out alone, but surely that was for business meetings, though thinking on it now, the late hour for the meetings was questionable. Had the gaming houses been his destination, and, oh goodness, did her mother know?

A loud clearing of a throat brought her back from her thoughts, and she found to her dismay that she was staring straight at Mr Langley. How long had she sat, her mind so far away, with her eyes fixed unfortunately at his groin. Her face flushed red, and she turned her head back toward the fire.

"You appeared to be in a trance of some kind. Are you ill? Will this interfere with the agreement?"

"I am not ill," she retorted tartly, "I was merely lost in my own thoughts and to what agreement are you referring?" She snapped, bravado sneaking in as hostility lurked in her gaze.

"Ah, there she is," he countered back, "I knew this demure, shy and innocent act couldn't last for long. Spencer said you were a spitfire." He stood there with a huge grin of delight on his face. This was the game he'd been waiting to play, ever since Spencer had fallen in love and been humiliated by this alluring yet spite filled woman. This was payback time!

<u>**Chapter Three**</u>

Abigail was more confused than ever. Was this man crazy? Spencer who? What kind of agreement had her father made with this, this man, who spoke lunacy? And why was she suddenly feeling like she was some kind of prey, hunted down, netted and installed in this cage of a house? So many questions, it was dizzying, overwhelming!

"Show me my room," she said, voice commanding. "I'm too weary, we shall finish this conversation in the morning. Nothing you say makes any sense. Tomorrow I shall make plans to return home, obviously whatever agreement that was made between you and my father shall have to be nullified."

"I don't think so," he drawled. "The agreement stands, you shall work off your father's debt, tomorrow you will be up early, with breakfast ready for when I rise. This way, Miss Dumont," he said with a mocking bow of his head as he pushed open the door, "your bed chamber awaits."

Abigail, taken aback, had no response. She squared her tired shoulders and moved with as much grace as her poor leg would allow, pulling her shoe back over her bare foot. Gritting her teeth, determined not to reveal to this beastly man how painful the burn was, she walked without a limp through the doorway with Mr Langley close behind her.

Oil lamps on the two hall tables lit the way along the passageway, the light from the flickering flame danced along the walls. Abigail slowly moved down the hallway toward the staircase, when his loud voice almost in her ear startled her. "In here." He reached around her and pushed open a door, then giving her a slight nudge forward he closed it behind her.

She waited, shock rooting her to the spot for a good long minute, her ear straining, listening for the click of a lock, but there was nothing. Once she realized she was alone, and he hadn't locked her in, she peered around, the small near-dark room. There was no oil lamp to help her see her way, merely a candle in its holder, left on a table beside the thin cot-like bed, a quarter of the size of her spacious mattress at home. She was grateful to note that her trunk had been deposited at the foot of the bed but overall, the space was uninspiring. Was this a servant's room? Had he really brought her here to work in his kitchen, as a maid? How had her father gotten everything so wrong?

A loud thud echoed in the hallway behind the closed door, and she jumped, a tiny squeak sounded from her lips, her hand rising to splay across her chest as she spun back around to face the door.

What now, surely, he wasn't coming back? A loud rap on the wood, then his voice "your other bag, Miss Dumont." The sound of his footsteps moving away down the hallway had her stepping to the door and slowly turning the handle. The door creaked open, and she stuck her head out, looking this way and that, checking, before leaning down and collecting her belongings then quickly backing up and shutting the door firmly once more. Moving to the bed she deposited her bag and coat on the coverlet and picked up the candle. And made her way back to the door to check for a key, surely there was a way to lock herself away, but the keyhole was bare and there was no other way to secure the door. Looking around once more, she saw a chair and dragged it noisily across the floor, arranging it this way and that to find the best way to safeguard the door and finally settled it with the legs on an angle and the back nudged beneath the doorhandle; it wasn't perfect, but it was the best she was going to do. Back at the bedside, she placed her bag on the floor and pulled the coverlet down and crawled fully dressed onto the cold sheet. She sat with her back braced against the hard stone wall, knees drawn up and tucked the coverlet around her. Tugging her coat around her shoulders for extra warmth and with tears trekking her cheeks, she settled in and watched the door.

Chapter Four

Edward stared out of his window. Without a moon, the moor was nothing but an abyss, the darkness an intense void. He used to be frightened of looking outside when he was a child, but now the darkness helped sooth him, well, usually it did. He moved to the fireplace, poked the embers and wondered again what Miss Dumont was doing, was she asleep, was she crying? Or was she plotting her escape?

The evening hadn't gone to plan at all, as was obvious by his now constant toing and froing between his bed and the fireplace, he was pacing! He never paced he thought and moved to the chair and slumped onto the cushion. What was it about this woman? Maybe he hadn't thought this plan through as well as he ought and damn her father for his underhandedness. Telling the lass she would be his wife, "not in this lifetime or the next," he growled. As if he would ever betray his cousin that way. But what was he to do now, the plan had been simple. Bring her here, make the little troublemaker pay for her poor actions. Teach her a lesson in humiliation so that when he returned her to society, she would be begging Spencer to take her back.

He'd thought it a stroke of luck when he'd encountered Mr Dumont at the gaming house. Where he'd sat listening to the mans slurred ramblings regarding his daughter and her failing engagement. Edward's ear had not been a sympathetic one; instead, the insistent prattle only fuelled Edwards anger. It seemed, Miss Dumont was on a roll of breaking men, Spencer and now her father too.

He was doing this for Spencer! His poor cousin had succumbed to the siren's call and fallen head over arse for the damn woman and where had that gotten him. Humiliated, broken. Edward couldn't stand by and do nothing; he would ring the bloody wench's neck if he could. His thoughts strayed to when he'd last seen Spencer.

His cousin had looked thin and drawn when Edward had visited. As much as Edward detested spending time in society, when his cousin, who was more like a brother, wrote him, he had responded immediately by making his way to London. He'd sat silent whilst Spencer spoke about the love of his life,

"Oh, cousin, Miss Dumont, has bewitched me, even now suffering through my humiliation, I can't get her out of my mind. I love her so, and must have her for my bride, I must. Yet she will not receive me when I call, and I fear, she will reject our engagement!"

He'd gone on to tell Edward all about their meeting and what went so very wrong.

"I first saw her at a dance," he said *"and was instantly attracted. I requested a dance, and as I held her hand, touched her waist and we moved about the dancefloor, I just knew she was the one for me. I was smitten! With each encounter I fell further in love with my little enchantress, bewitched by her red hair and green eyes, she was flirtatious, and fun, would not stand for rude behaviour and quite the spitfire if she thought people were out of line. She's not stiff and proper like the other young ladies who attend the balls and parties, and when I suggested a turn round the garden, she was forward in removing her glove so we could hold hands. My infatuation hit a new level, and I blurted out my intention of making her my wife and she laughed at me."*

"What? She laughed, was she not interested in your advances then?" Edward had interrupted. Spencer held up a hand to silence him.

"Oh yes, she was interested. She told me that she'd fallen in love with me the moment we met, and her laughter was relief and joy that I felt the same, then with no further words, she leaned in, and she kissed me, and I was drowning; instead of fighting to come up for air, I sank deeper. Miss Dumont's lips are seductive, once tasted." Spencer had fallen silent for a long moment, lost in the memory of the taste of her lips. "Now that she was certain of my intent, any acts of propriety vanished, and Edward, I shouldn't kiss and tell, but she was magnificent."

Edward frowned, "I don't understand, if she was happy to wed you and was gratified by your advances then why do you feel humiliated? Spence, what haven't you told me?" He knew his cousin well enough to know there must be more to the story than a laughing bride to be, or a bit of pre-marital hanky-panky, but then again, he'd never felt inclined to take a wife, love was not for him.

"Well," Spencer continued, "I wasn't about to lift her skirts in the garden, was I? As much as I wanted to. My plan was to carry her away to my house but as we moved to go back inside to collect her coat, the lights illuminated the high pink flush of her cheeks, and her lip colouring smudged from out kisses and I knew I must keep her hidden, away from prying eyes and wagging tongues, and so we gained accessed via a darkened room off the balcony."

"Spencer, anyone could have seen you, her reputation would be ruined before you had a chance to wed her."

Spencer grimaced. "Exactly why I was trying to hide the evidence of our desire and, well, as it turned out, it was my reputation that was to be questioned. Being alone with her was a bad call, because once the door was closed, I couldn't keep my hands off her. Before I knew it, my trousers were unbuttoned and my hands were pushing her gown up her thighs, such satiny thighs," he sighed. "Her scent, like honey, I can still ..."

"No," Edward raised his hand, stopping him. "I do not need to hear the details; Facts man, I just need facts."

"Well, I was so caught up in the moment, Edward, that when a cough sounded behind me, just as I was about to enter her, the interruption shocked both me and my aim, and my misguided thrust knocked at her, um, other entrance," he grimaced as he recalled it, "and she screamed, and I hastily withdrew."

"Well, I see why you might be a tad humiliated old boy, but still."

"No," Spencer interrupted this time. "That was just the beginning. The cough came from non-other than Lord Dandion who appeared right behind me, hands on my shoulders, hauling me away from my screaming fiancé, and I fell back against him."

"Oh, no. Not him." Edward groaned.

"There's more, Edward. My darling girl was frantic that we'd been observed, and with Lord Dandion at my back and holding me; add to that my miscalculated aim, and well, she put two and two together and came up with something truly outrageous. I could scare believe what I heard, she was furious, hissing over my shoulder at Dandion, 'about my preference to bugger than tup' and then she looked at me,

standing with my trousers around my knees, at the man behind me, and I saw; I saw the moment her eyes widened, that she had concluded the worst, 'you're together!' she admonished.

"No, she did not? She thought you were a couple, what did you do?" Edward asked.

"Well, I'm sorry to say that in the heat of the moment, and the embarrassment I felt at her words, they..." Spencer shook his head; "I was blindsided, and I didn't think. Instead of covering her up and proclaiming my love was for her and her alone, I backed away, unfortunately further into Dandions embrace and I felt how much he was enjoying the show. She began to cry as she dragged her gown down and turning, threw open the doors and charged out into the hallway, her face tear streaked and deathly pale. Of course, I followed, more slowly as I struggled to pull up my trousers, my face as red as a beet; and the grand finale to our act was a beaming Lord Dandion hot on my tail. He's twice since invited me to join his hunting party.

The rumours started the following day, that I was caught with Lord Dandion in the library. And now Miss Dumont will not receive me when I visit. I'm sure she will no longer agree to..."

"Nobody saw you leave that room?" Edward interrupted.

"No, I don't believe so, there was nobody in the hallway at all, it was just the three of us. How can I win back h...?"

"Stop! I think I've heard quite enough."

Edward had never met the woman, hadn't even heard of her until Spencer appeared, broken and humiliated.

And now, Edward was out for blood She would pay for the ugly untruth she had spread about his cousin. He'd bring this ruthless gossip to her knees. He would humiliate her as she had Spencer with her insinuation of his sexual preference and with Lord Dandion of all people. He'd teach her a lesson for playing with his cousin feelings, he would take her down a peg and then she would go begging to his cousin to take her back.

And yet, as he'd stood in the doorway watching Miss Dumont in his forecourt earlier, his fingers itching to steal around her neck as he worked to keep his anger in check; he couldn't help but feel a strange kind of pull to the cursed chit. She had looked so young, so lost and vulnerable, that he'd physically shaken his head to clear the feeling away. If she had this much power over her men, was even he safe from her wiles? Hell, he'd almost fallen for that helpless act as she'd sat afront the fire, her innocence was all very believable. The clumsiness, the fear during her fall had almost been his undoing and then, she'd turned on him, her eyes spitting fire and he saw a much different version of Miss Dumont; she was indeed a spitfire when angered and he found that attracted him all the more. How many facets did one woman hold? He'd felt the need to tame her one moment, coddle her the next, the feelings were damned dizzying and to top it all off, as he'd administered to her burns, he'd felt protective of her, that was until he'd run his fingertips along the extremely soft skin, wishing he could brush higher and higher up her thigh, his cock hardening instantly, and suddenly it wasn't protective that he was feeling, but lust, he'd wanted to take her there and then on his dining table.

Damn it all to hell, he was pacing again.

<u>Chapter Five</u>

Jackson growled when he entered the dark, cold kitchen in the early hours of the morning and found no breakfast awaited him.

Had the woman overslept or had the master changed his mind about the lady working in the kitchen. Why was she working anyway? Jackson was confused he had seen her home, she wasn't from an impoverished family, didn't need a wage. She'd not said too much during the long journey from London, and she never complained about the discomfort she must have felt being jostled around the carriage for nigh on four days or spoken a bad word during their nights staying at Inn's along the way. She was subdued, a little nervous. Miss Dumont had been polite to everybody, the Inn keepers, the wait staff from kitchen and dining, and even to the stable boys, she'd offered a polite smile, nod of her head and a thank you.

Jackson crossed to the hearth and stoked the fire, blowing on the embers until smoke rose and they glowed orange, added pinecones and wood bark and waited for them to catch, and then taking a shovel of glowing embers from the base, he moved across and deposited them into the firebox of the cast iron stove, adding wood and coal, then settling the large copper kettle atop the range.

The master would be wanting some nice hot water to wash when he arose, and Miss Dumont too, he would imagine. Once he had seen to the fires, he lit the lamps taking one in hand he moved quietly down the hall to where he'd delivered Miss Dumont's belongings and gently tap, tap, tapped on the door. Pressing his ear to the wood panelling, he listened carefully for any sound and when nothing was forthcoming, he knocked again a tad louder and whisper shouted, "Miss Dumont, are ye awake? It's time ye were up and, in the kitchen. Miss Dumont? Miss?" He heard shuffling footsteps crossing the room, the door didn't open, but her voice came through.

"It's still dark, I've not yet slept. It can't be time to rise," she insisted.

"Aye, Miss, tiz early and dark, but tiz past the time for ye to be in the kitchen and seeing to breakfast."

He stood back as he heard a dragging sound, wondering what she was about, and then the door swung inward and there stood a very bedraggled looking Abigail, her hair tousled, her gown torn, rumpled and grubby.

Jackson stared in dismay, what on earth had the master done to her? A ripped gown, no, no Mr Langley was a gentleman, a kind-hearted man; Sure, he could be a little hard when angered, but he wouldn't have done this to the poor girl.

"My apologies for waking you, Miss," Jackson said.

"No, the apology is mine," Miss Dumont murmured, "for my tardiness and for the state of my attire," she added, noticing Jackson's shocked face. "Is there water where I may freshen up? Mr Langley was not hospitable enough last night to address my toilet, a quite unforgivable sin and obvious testimony to the type of man he is."

Jackson had never heard his master spoken of in quite this way before, it irked him, but seeing the little miss's discomfort, he had to wonder.

"Aye, I've put the kettle on, I'll fill yer basin and help ye out a little this morning, seein' as ye've not slept none.

There should be a pot under the bed for ye needs in the night, and the outhouse is out back, I'll show ye once the master has breakfasted."

"Thank you, Jackson, for your kindness."

"Have ye made a breakfast afore Miss?" he asked, "Cos the master will be about soon enough and will be calling for his food."

"The master will just have to wait then; the insufferable man won't starve if his meal is on the table a little late."

Jackson's eyes widened almost comically as she spoke. Mr Langley wasn't a difficult man, but he did like his meals on the table on time. He was a good man, kind to his staff. Every Christmas he gave them a fortnight off from their duties, to visit their families, leaving only himself, who had no family, to watch the animals.

A loud whistle had him hurrying back to the kitchen. He added another log on the fire and a second shovel of coal to the stove's fire box, grabbed the thick cloth from a hook beside the stove and hoisted the whistling kettle up off the heat and the room grew instantly silent. Pouring the boiling water into a basin then adding cold water and a washcloth, he trudged back along the hallway and with a nod from Abigail, deposited it on the chair which stood beside the door.

"Thank you," Abigail said and closed the door behind him.

Jackson moved back to the kitchen and began rounding up bread, butter and ham and then sat back to eat his fill of his late breakfast.

<u>**Chapter Six**</u>

Abigail was tired! She hadn't dared to close her eyes throughout the night, her ears straining for the tiniest of sounds. Worrying that every creak the old house made would bring another frustrating encounter with Mr Langley.

Her brain felt thick and gloopy from lack of sleep and from traversing the same useless thought path all night. What was she doing here? Was she really expected to be a maid? Was her father truly visiting a gaming house, and if so, how much trouble was he in? Was this arrangement with Mr Langley a way to pay off a debt? Her heart ached when she remembered her father standing by the door, watching as Bernard, their butler, squirreled her away in the awaiting carriage. Surely, he must understand that by not having a maid accompany her, her reputation was in very real danger. No gentleman would offer for her if it was known she was in a man's home with no chaperone. She would be ruined!

With no tears left to spill, she took a deep shuddering breath and decided, whatever Mr Langley threw her way, she would get through it, she would not be broken.

She had jumped almost out of her skin when the soft tap, tapping came at her door. She'd pulled the covers up higher, waiting to see if Mr Langley would push his way into her room. But the voice calling from behind her door was that of the stable hand, who had been so very kind to her during the journey here.

And it seems his kindness would continue as he set the basin of hot water down on her chair, she thanked him and closed the door.

Abigail plunged her hands into the hot water and closed her eyes, so warm, so very warm. Her fingers had been almost numb from the night spent in this icy cold room, now the delicious heat seeped into her fingertips and rose higher up her palms to her wrists. What wouldn't she give for her bathtub in which to submerge her entire body. She ached from her long journey and the uncomfortable bed in which she'd sat all night.

She stood naked, shivering in the near dark room, the only light coming from the small crack beneath her door. The tiny stub of candle left from last night long burnt out, her ruined gown discarded on the floor and her under garments piled to one side, she dipped the rough cloth again and again as she washed, refreshing her body with the quickly cooling water. With care she dabbed, cleansing the blisters that had formed on her leg overnight, biting her lip to withhold the whimpers as she accidently rubbed too hard the raw flesh surrounding them. Damn it, she could barely see what she was doing.

Shivering violently now, she opened her trunk, drew out clean undergarments and another of the dowdy gowns, her mother had her maid pack. Had that been a missed clue? Did her mother know something?

She dressed as quickly as she could, finding it difficult to button the bodice of her gown with shaking fingers, pulled up one stocking and secured it with a garter, but decided against pulling up her other, instead, rolling it to sit bulky at her ankle, leaving the burns free of coverings She uncoiled her hair, ran a brush through the heavy strands and then circled it back up into a knot the best she could with no mirror or maid to assist.

Squaring her shoulders, she opened the door, and taking the basin of grimy water with her, marched her way toward the light down the hallway and into the kitchen.

"Good morning, Jackson, thank you for your kindness this morning, could you tell me where I can dispose of this? She asked indicating the basin she carried.

"Aye, Miss, give it 'ere I'll do that for ye." Placing his bread back on the plate, he stood, strode across the kitchen and took the heavy basin from her hands, "a basin full can go down the sink here in the kitchen, a full bath, now that goes outside." He chatted away whilst he emptied the basin for her.

"Thank you." She stood wringing her hands, unsure of what to do next. "Have you worked here very long?"

"Aye, Miss. I've known the Master since he was knee high to a grasshopper, he was a right mischief maker as a lad."

"Hmm, seems he's not changed too much then," Abigail said. "I wonder what mischief he thinks he's dabbling in by stealing me away from my home."

"Oh, Miss, ye'll be quite safe with Mr Langley, he's a proper gentleman ye know. I understand there's an agreement tween your father and him, as to why ye're staying a bit."

"My Father gave me the impression that I am to wed your Master, Jackson," she said bluntly, "but it seems Mr Langley has different ideas. Maybe you would be so kind as to assist me..."

"I can't be doing anythin' behind the Master's back now, Miss. His business is his own, and so long as nobody's hurt, I'll be keepin' me nose to meself," Jackson was quick to interrupt.

"Oh, I would never ask you to betray your Master, but you must see, my being here is wrong. There is no concern for me in this arrangement. I feel I've been duped, Jackson. Lied to, led to believe I'd be mistress of the house yet find I'm to work here as a maid."

"Well, Miss, an agreement is an agreement, I'm not saying it's right, but..." he shrugged. "I can show ye where things are in the kitchen if ye want, then Mr Langley can have his breakfast and leave ye in peace, most days he'll ride out to check the beasties, especially this time of the year with the weather so changeable."

"So, he's a farmer then? What do you farm? Cows, Sheep?" she pushed for more information on her jailer.

"Aye, Miss. We have some cows and sheep, but with Mr Langley it's all about the horses, he spends a fair amount of his time at the stables. We have some of the best breeding stock," he said, pride filling his voice.

After a brief tour of the kitchen, reminding her to keep the two fires burning, he excused himself to get on with his own work.

Abigail slowly moved around the kitchen, she gaped at the vast amount of food when she opened the door in the corner of the room and finding a walk-in larder. She ogled the preserves, jar upon jars filled the shelves. She unwrapped muslin cloth and discovered they held an assortment of bread, meats and wheels of cheese. There were tins filled with delicious looking cakes, biscuits and thick crusted pies. Baskets of potatoes and other vegetables. If Mr

Langley had no staff, then who on earth had prepared the feast hidden in his kitchen?

Abigail's parents may be gentry and had their own serving staff, but Abigail was no stranger in the kitchen. She'd spent hours as a child and young adult visiting with Bessie, their cook, who'd always had a welcoming hug and had insisted on teaching her how to make her favourite sweets. Those had been some of Abigail's happiest memories, the warmth she'd felt in the kitchen had created a safe and friendly space when her parents and siblings had little time for her.

Abigail looked around the big kitchen, and felt that familiar warmth in her chest, she'd make Bessie proud. She got to work checking the firebox and shovelling in another scoop of coal. Placing the heavy skillet on the hot plate to heat, she added butter and then cracked in the eggs. She busied herself cutting slabs of bread and slathered them in butter, cut hefty slices of ham before chopping two tomatoes and half a dozen mushrooms and added them to the skillet, moving the eggs around a little so they didn't stick while she waited for them to cook.

On a tray, she positioned a cup and saucer, scooped milk from the pail into a jug, placing it and a bowl of sugar next to it, then added boiling water to the teapot, leaning forward to watch as the black specs of tea rose and floated in the steaming water. Back at the range, she checked on the eggs, tomatoes and mushrooms then set to arranging the bread, and plated eggs atop the ham and decorated the plate with glistening red tomato and succulent, juicy mushrooms. She stood back admiring her handywork, yes, Bessie would be proud. A smile touched her lips and as a tear welled, a bittersweet moment, she blinked it away. Pulling her shoulders back, she lifted the tray and left the safety of the kitchen, she took a deep breath and entered the dining room.

<u>**Chapter Seven**</u>

Edward turned, looking over his shoulder from his crouched position, his gaze landing on Miss Dumont as she entered the room. His eyes raked her, taking in every tiny detail as he rose to standing before the fireplace, the smouldering logs all but forgotten as he stared at the woman, saw her slight hesitation when she noticed him, then she continued forward toward the dining table.

Her attire this morning was as drab as it had been yesterday, and he wondered what she'd look like if dressed in the beautiful gowns she likely wore at home or to parties. She had pulled her hair into a knot atop her head, same as how she'd worn it last evening, but this morning there were runaway whisps of auburn that had escaped their pins and curled enticingly around her pinkened cheeks, no doubt caused by the heat from the stove. She was beautiful and he found himself moving with no actual thought towards where she bent forward slightly, lowering the tray, setting the table place for his breakfast.

The temptation to touch her was so powerful. He stopped close enough that he could feel the heat of her body radiating through her gown, warming him, in the frigidly cold room. Felt as much as heard the breathy inward gasp as she sensed him behind her and her body stilled for a just a moment, before she straightened, moving that delicious bottom away from the hardly-there touch of his groin.

His whispered breath stirred the escaped auburn whisps and he noted the tiny goosebumps appear along her forearms, and then she turned, hips slightly grazing his front, and it was his turn to pull in a shuddering breath; then she was facing him, her eyes level with his neck before gradually climbing to capture his eyes. His gaze broke away first, lowering to note the hard peaks of her breasts as they rose and fell, with her quickening breath. Eyes still on his face, she sidestepped, and his gaze fell to the table where only last night he'd sat with her spread like a feast in front of him. Damn, what was she doing to him? His brain addled, his own breathing ragged in his chest and his cock was hard against the buttons of his pants. He cleared his throat.

"You surprise me, Miss Dumont. Here I was expecting burnt offerings at best." He stepped closer to the table, keeping his betraying body parts turned away from her and slipped into his seat.

Silence.

"Cat got your tongue?" he queried.

She continued to sidle toward the door, her eyes never leaving him, as she backed away like prey having wandered to close to a predator's lair and was now waiting for the attack.

"You are not yet dismissed," he said. She stilled mere steps from freedom. "Silence does not become you, Miss Dumont, surely a simple good morning is not too much to ask."

"Good morning," she ground out dropping her gaze to her hands now clasped in front of her. She could feel his eyes and was determined not to give in to the need to fidget. Keeping her head bowed, hiding her overly expressive face from his perusal. She couldn't let him see how her fingers itched to scratch and tear, and her toes curled in her boots just waiting to kick. Yet she stood statue still!

Moments passed and finally he spoke, "This is quite a feast you've prepared; it seems I've underestimated your abilities in the kitchen."

Her head snapped up, and she gave him a withering look that clearly said she didn't appreciate his condescending tone.

"I've spent many enjoyable hours in a kitchen, Mr Langley. Now, maybe you'd like to finish eating before it goes cold. I have work to do." Ah, the little spitfire in her popped up again, and then she was back to a controlled silence as she walked away, leaving him to watch as her hips swayed, and grinning to himself when he realized she'd defied him, the minx, because he still hadn't dismissed her.

What was the young chit playing at he wondered as he pulled his chair flush to the table, exactly how he'd done last night but with a totally different feast set before him. The mental picture of those satiny thighs, that had kept him up for much of the night, came to mind. He shook the thoughts free and began to eat the delicious breakfast set before him. She was a fine cook, and that posed a slight snag in his, let's face it, not so well thought out plan. She wasn't supposed to enjoy any part of her punishment; she was meant to be miserable, sullying her hands, embarrassed when she failed at the menial task and humiliated when he scoffed at her burnt offerings. He hadn't for a moment imagined she would enjoy spending time in a kitchen.

Edward took his time with his meal. He was enjoying a second cup of tea when Abigail appeared in the doorway, obviously surprised to find him still seated.

"Miss Dumont, that was exceptional. You may clear away and then take time to break your own fast. Tomorrow,

I think, coffee instead of tea." He rose to his feet, nudged the now burning logs with the toe of his boot and said, "I'll be in my study. Find me there in half an hour to discuss your daily chores."

Abigail's eyes narrowed, but she acknowledged with a simple nod and began packing the dirty dishes onto the tray, then squaring her shoulders, feeling his eyes follow her, she left the room without a word. The man infuriated her. But, until she could find a way home, she would keep her thoughts to herself and play the part of a dutiful servant; barely seen, rarely heard; she could do this!

Chapter Eight

Half an hour later found Abigail standing in the cold hallway wondering which of the closed doors would lead her to the study. She tapped lightly on the door nearest, holding her breath as she listened for a response. Nothing. She moved to the next and tap, tap. Still nothing. This was ridiculous, her temper flared, this man was turning her into an insipid little mouse. "Mr Langley," she called loudly and wrapped her knuckles noisily on the wall closest to her. She waited and was rewarded when further down the hall a door swung open and Edward stepped out, his arms folded as he glowered at her. Okay, so maybe she couldn't play the silent dutiful maid after all.

"Ah, there you are Mr Langley."

Abigail hurried along the passage and walked past the menacing figure and into his study. Damn the man! She was here to work off a monetary debt, by no fault of her own; she'd done no wrong and she would not be made to cower. She was Abigail Dumont, strong and independent. He would not change her into a simpering, frightened little girl. She was a lady, well-educated. Mr Langley would learn quickly, that, whilst she held up her father's end of the arrangement; she would not be walked over and would demand to be treated with the respect she deserved during the duration of her incarceration.

She seated herself in front of his desk and waited for him to move from the doorway. He didn't.

"Miss Dumont," the words were growled. "A knock on the door is customary when attempting to gain entrance or attention."

She turned, "Mr Langley, if you had given direction, I would have knocked on your door. Instead, I found myself in a maze, your home is not small, Sir and I did knock at more than one of the doors, to no avail. It seemed less time consuming to call out to you, and it appears my surmise was correct."

Edward's eyebrows rose at her words, 'game on, Miss Dumont' he thought. He stood silently, waiting, his expression hard until finally relenting he spoke again. "Now that you have found me, might I point out that 'the help' waits to be invited into a room, and stands whilst orders are given." He stopped speaking, once more waiting for her to stand, to follow his *suggestion*. Her only response was to fold her hands demurely into her lap, eyes raised to his. A stand-off!

"Miss Dumont," he spat, stalking toward her, angry that he was the one to break first. "Your chores as listed; cooking, I require three meals a day, breakfast, luncheon and dinner. There is washing, cleaning, filling of the oil lamps and fires to attend. You are a servant in this house and as such will speak to me when spoken to, you will see to the chores I assign and you will treat me with respect like any employee to their employer, am I making myself quite clear?" If he was waiting for her to meekly nod and 'yes sir' his words, he was to be sorely disappointed.

Abigail rose and took one long step towards him, enough to invade his space. Eyes flashing angrily, she answered loudly without a tremor and the tone cutting. "You have made yourself abundantly clear! And yet I find myself unable to comply to your ... commands. Firstly, I am not an employee, Mr Langley. An employee gets paid a wage, whereas I do not. Doing menial tasks to pay a debt, does not make me a servant, merely a pawn in your game; to my father a chess piece easily, it seems, sacrificed in payment of his stupidity, but in your case, Mr Langley, I'm nothing more than a trophy piece.

I shall, however, being the dutiful daughter that I am, agree to uphold the agreement, which I would like to see, and I shall do such menial tasks that you request. But remember, Mr Langley, I am not a servant. I am a lady and shall be treated as such. I will not cower to you and your animalistic growling." She raised a hand as he opened his mouth, and he quickly closed it again as she continued.

"On the other hand, you, are no gentleman. A gentleman wouldn't take a woman as payment for a debt. A true gentleman, Mr Langley would have thought about the consequences of keeping an unwed lady locked away without a maid, or chaperone of any kind. A gentleman wouldn't ruin a lady's reputation as mine shall surely be if it is discovered that I am here alo..." His hands moved in a blur as they moved to clasp her shoulders and then his lips slammed over hers, effectively shutting her ranting down. She froze. He was kissing her! Shock replaced her anger, and something else, which she couldn't name, as his mouth moved over hers, coaxing a compliance. Her hands which had been balled into fists during her showdown, unclenched at her sides as a different form of adrenaline coursed through her and her fingers itched once more to make contact, thought this time not to injure, she pushed them against the hard wall of his chest, not hard enough to move him, just to feel, a place to anchor as her head swam. The hands clutching her shoulders softened as he pulled her closer still, travelling down her back to trap her in his embrace as the kiss deepened and her lips parted on a sigh.

"Edward, Jackson let me ...oh... my apologies." A tall man stopped just inside the open doorway. But instead of beating a hasty retreat to leave the two their privacy, he made himself comfortable, leaning against the doorframe and took in the sight with interest.

Edward abruptly released Abigail lips, but still held her to him, dazedly with a whispered curse he turned to the intruder. "Francis, you're early. I was just ..." he stepped in front of Abigail knowing his friend would note his obvious arousal, it wasn't easy to hide, but with her words still ringing in his ears, he felt compelled to at least attempt to shield her from his friend's prying eyes.

"Just?" Francis queried, then grinned. "Yes, I'm a little early. I know we agreed to meet at the stables Edward, but I thought we could partake in a ride before business," he grinned salaciously, before adding, "but it seems maybe I'm too late, or maybe a tad early...for riding." He peered around Edward's shoulder and eyed Abigail bowed head with interest. With a quietly muttered "Excuse me," she scurried, head still lowered toward the door.

<u>**Chapter Nine**</u>

The horses worried at their bit, their mouth's frothing as they fought to slow their breathing in the freezing, winter air. Their hooves danced on the frozen ground, pawing at the icy white tips of grass and heather that covered this part of the moor. Sweat glistened on their coats, the men had ridden them hard and fast, only slowing now for a moment of rest before turning their mounts back toward the stables.

Edward had given Francis no time to question. He'd quickly followed Abigail from the study, his friend close on his heels and made for the front door, enveloping his body in the burly coat that Jackson handed him. His body still hummed from his embrace with Miss Dumont and the warmth of the coat only added to his already hot and aching body. He could scarcely breath as he'd hurried outside and felt the blessed cold air on his exposed skin, his heated face and he looked skyward for a moment as if checking for bad weather, but really giving himself a few seconds to compose himself, and then followed Francis who had already mounted and was now staring down at him.

Placing his foot in the stirrup, he'd hoisted himself into the saddle and without a second glance in Francis's directions, squeezed his knees into his stallion's sides, the horse danced a couple of dainty steps before breaking into a gallop.

The frigid air made breathing painful, as both Edward and Francis leant over to pat and stroke the glistening necks of the beautiful beasts beneath them. They sat a while, giving the horses a moment to catch their second wind, and were treated to a breathtaking scene as the dark clouds parted and the sun bestowed its light and warmth to the frosted ground, lighting the icy crystals and making them shimmer like a chest of jewels, a priceless treasure to behold.

"Are you going to tell me who she is?" Francis asked finally.

"No," Edward replied crisply.

"No? Why on earth not? You seemed rather cosy with each other. I thought I knew all your close friends; I'm pretty sure I would have remembered an introduction to such a rare beauty."

There mounts fidgeted, eyes rolling a little in panic as a scream echoed through the still air. "It's just a fox, boy," Francis murmured, calming his horse.

Edward frowned, glancing back to where they'd come, then nudged his horse to walk on and replied. "She's not a close friend," dismissing the look on his friends face that said quite plainly that they certainly seemed close. "She is nobody. Just a maid," and then cursed silently to himself; that was a mistake, damn, once he released her from this short-term arrangement, she would return to town, partake in societies activities and attend the parties which Francis would undoubtedly be invited to. Shit, shit, shit.

"Since when do you tup your maids, Edward? Although I admit if she worked for me, I'd appreciate her being on my *staff*," he raised and lowered his eyebrows, "pun totally intended," he chuckled to himself, well pleased at his clever innuendo.

Edward glowered. "Don't speak of her like that, in fact don't speak of her at all. And, I am not, tupping my maid."

"No, maybe not, but you were well on the way when I walked in. Where did you find such a delectable chit, I want one," he said pouting like a spoiled child. "Or maybe, I can take yours if you don't want her?"

Edward growled, rolled his eyes and with a gently nudge of his heels he urged his mount into a canter. Francis Fletcher already had a wife at home and any number of lovers for when he visited London, he certainly didn't need another anything. Edward would say nothing more on the matter of Miss Dumont, Francis was already too interested and the more said, the more interest he would take.

Arriving back at the house, Jackson took the reins and led the horses back toward the stables, whilst the gentlemen moved indoors, removing their outer wear and heading for the study. Edward's gaze searching, ever watchful for his new 'employee'.

Once inside, with the door closed firmly behind them, he produced the documents of sale and Francis signed it with a flourish, then shaking his head signed the second sheaf of papers Edward set before him. He'd come to buy the chestnut filly for his wife, a Christmas gift, but hadn't been able to resist the grey gelding he'd just taken out for a run, the grey would make a fine addition to his stable.

"Will Jackson and Tristan bring them over?" he asked as he lay the pen on the jotter, ink leaking from its tip.

"Er, when were you thinking?" Edward asked as he picked the fountain pen up and replaced the lid, mumbling curses as his fingers stained blue.

"Sunday is Christmas Eve; I think that would work perfectly. I won't have trouble hiding her gift for one night, and if Mrs Fletcher sees your men, I can simply tell her they were delivering my new gelding."

Edward frowned, "I don't think I can spare Jackson this week. With my staff on Christmas leave, Tristan included, I'm down to only Jackson and Mis.. um the new maid until after the holiday. Would it be possible to send your men instead?"

"You know, I've never understood why your family let the staff off over Christmas and not just give them Boxing day, like the rest of us. But in this case, it works to my advantage. I'll come with Seymour and lead them home in time for Christmas. It will give me a second peak at your delectable new staff member; speaking of which, what treats can your delightful redhead pull together; I'm feeling a tad peckish."

Edward frowned; this was a bad idea! Miss Dumont wasn't meant to be seen, which was the reason he'd organised to meeting Francis at the stables, now he was stuck. He didn't intend to subject Miss Dumont to any of Francis' shenanigans, but how to say no without being rude to his friend and buyer. "Make yourself comfortable," he gestured to the chairs before the blazing fire, "I'll go and see what can be rustled up."

"I take it your call-bell is broken, Edward." He grinned as Edward turned with an agitated look on his face, "no, go, I'm just being facetious, I wouldn't dare be the cause of your blue balls a second time; go, have your little tête-à-tête with your scrumptious little maid, I'll just pour myself some of your best whiskey," he winked, and Edward shook his head and left the room. This whole business seemed to be spiralling out of his control.

<u>Chapter Ten</u>

Abigail was furious! At whom it was directed she wasn't entirely sure. Mr Langley, she supposed earned most of her ire, kissing her as he had, to shut her up. But she herself deserved a good talking to for allowing his lips to linger, she shouldn't have stood so long or enjoyed the sensation so much. "Hateful man!" she groaned to herself; she hated him! Didn't she?

It was humiliating how easily she had surrendered, her cheeks burned with mortification, at being caught in Mr Langley's embrace. Who was that man? Obviously, an acquaintance or more probably a friend, as Jackson had allowed the man to enter without being escorted or announced. Oh, God, what must he think? And what would Mr Langley tell him? Surely, he would keep her name to himself. She bowed her head, eyes prickling with unshed tears; her life was over if he named and shamed her; her reputation would be lost. She sniffled. Tears slipped from between her long lashes, and Abigail didn't even try to stop them. She would be ruined!

The kitchen was warm and almost comforting, and she dearly wished Bessie was here to talk to, she missed her dreadfully. With her much-loved cook in mind, Abigail moved to the sink, emptying the water from the kettle and adding some cold, she washed down the table and scrubbed the cutting block, then refilled the big kettle setting it back atop the burner to boil. The kitchen was spotlessly clean and tidy, and Abigail felt an overwhelming sense of pride in her morning achievements; if nothing else, she had shown she could cook a meal and clean a kitchen. Her face fell, and quite possibly ruined her entire life whilst experiencing her first ever kiss.

Glancing out the window, she watched as the two men rode away from the house. Maybe she should leave, put on her coat and run away? But hadn't she just told Mr Langley that she was a dutiful daughter and would comply to the arrangement made? But how could she stay? She ran her fingers over her lips, the feeling of Mr Langley's mouth lingered, but then again, how could she leave? She was so conflicted.

The least she could do was find out where she was. All Abigail knew, was she had travelled four days West of her home. Returning to her room, she buttoned her coat, effectively covering her dowdy gown, and pulled on her gloves, smoothing the leather over each slender digit. She would use the front entrance she decided, not wishing to run into Jackson in case he tried to stop her from leaving.

Stepping through the front door, Abigail pulled in her first deep breath of freedom; the inhalation caused her to cough a little as her lungs expanded and filled with frigid air. Venturing forward to where the carriage had stopped last evening, she stood, looking around, her thoughts on the latter part of her journey. Remembering how quiet the road had been, no other conveyance passing; maybe the cold and the early nightfall of winter had driven the neighbours inside early.

There had been no noise, because there were no neighbours. Nothing could have prepared her for the bleak, lonely landscape that met her eyes. "No, no, no" she cried as she spun in a slow circle, the house she'd just escaped sat alone, a monstrous jail in the middle of a desolate terrain.

She'd never seen the likes, where the devil was she? An eerie mist hovered just above her knees, shrouding the land like a ghostly bolt of shimmering silk, it undulated and swirled like a slow-moving whirlpool. The ground was impossible to see, what horrors were harboured within? Abigail sucked in breath after breath, trying to quell her rising panic as the damp tendrils threaded themselves through her coat, her gown, and she screamed.

The sound of running footfalls filled the deathly silence following her cry. Oh god, what was coming? Her head was telling her to flee, her feet unable to comply. If she ran, what lay below waiting to trip her, to swallow her up. She was frozen by fear.

An arm closed around her shivering shoulders, a voice dragging her back from the yawning abyss her panicked mind had created, "I've got ye, Miss. Ye're safe."

Abigail turned her head, raising her face to stare at the kindly eyes of Jackson, his gaze flashed around them searching for what had caused her to scream. "What was it, Miss? What frightened ye?" he asked when he finally bought his gaze back to hers.

"Wh. What is this, where are we? I've never seen the likes before. There's nothing, it's like the world has disappeared, there's no life, no sound, just the, the..." she pointed toward the mist. "I've seen the fog in town, where entire houses seem to be swallowed whole, but I've never seen..." she swung her hand back and forward as if she didn't know what to call what she was seeing, couldn't explain the discomfort of not being able to see the ground whilst all around her, knee high and up the air was crisp, the sun blanketed behind light cloud.

"It's a common sight round these parts, the mist at half-mast. It'll clear once the wind picks up, or the clouds part, and then ye're in for a treat. The moor is a sight to behold when the sun shines. Come on inside, Miss, it's too cold to be standing out 'ere. Come on, and ye can tell me why ye're as skittish as the master's foals in a thunderstorm."

Moving his arm from her shoulder and gently easing her forward with a gentle pressure to her back, she allowed him to take her back to the house. Her body shook uncontrollably as he freed her of her coat and waited whilst she removed her gloves. "Come on, Miss, the fire is burning nicely in the dining room, why don't ye get warmed up and I'll bring ye in a nice cuppa tea."

Abigail sat, hands clenched on her lap, trying her best to regain her lost composure. To stop the shakes; To battle back the fear that had swarmed her like flies on manure, whilst she'd stood out in the mist. This was so unlike her. She never panicked! But here, the silence, the vastness so unsettled her. She still didn't know where she was, why there were no people, no houses. There was nothing, nowhere for her to run, nobody to turn to for assistance. Oh God, she really was trapped here! No escape unless she attempted to cross the mist covered moor with its hidden rocks, dips and trenches. There could be mineshafts, or wells into which one could fall and never be recovered. And what of the wildlife, were there dangerous creatures inhabiting the labyrinth of land that lay like a giant moat around this house. These thoughts were not calming her.

Jackson came back through the door with a cup rattling in its saucer and she turned her terrified gaze on him.

"Aw lass, I don't think tea is gonna do the trick," he moved to the decanter and poured the golden liquid into a glass and came to slowly crouch before her, "ere drink this."

She took the glass in shaking hands and sipped gratefully at the searing fluid, coughed and sipped again. "Where are we?"

"Cornwall, Miss, not far from Wadebridge. Way down the Southwest. That, out there is Bodmin Moor, there's a few cottages dotted ere and there, but nothing too close." He nudged the glass in her hand, "drink up, Miss. I think maybe ye're lack of sleep isn't helping ye non. An' ye've had quite the shock." He took the glass from her stiff fingers and replaced it with the cup and saucer and then left the room. She absently tipped the spilled liquid from her saucer back into the cup and took a deep sip, swallowing the hot tea; each sip calming her a little more. She placed the empty cup on the little table, glancing at the book that lay there, Nicholas Nickleby. She hadn't read it. Maybe she should, then she and Mr Langley may have something to converse over. She turned her gaze back to the flickering flames, skin warm and eyelids heavy. Perhaps she shouldn't have drunk the whiskey.

She didn't move when Jackson came in a few moments later, draped the blanket he'd bought in, over her slumbering body, and then placed another log quietly in the grate, lifted the cup and saucer and left the room, quietly closing the door behind him.

<u>**Chapter Eleven**</u>

Where the hell was she?

Edward had surged into the kitchen ready to, to what? Apologise? Sweep her back into his arms? No, that couldn't happen, ever again, she belonged to Spencer.

Certain that she had heard him coming down the hall, he moved to check the pantry, expecting to find her squeezed beneath a shelf or crouched behind a sack of flour, hiding from him. But no, she wasn't there. He didn't have all day to play hide-and-seek, Francis wouldn't sit idly for long. He grabbed a couple of tins that Evelyn, his cook, had left on the shelf and began to pile up a tray, cold cuts, pies, cakes and biscuits all jumbled together, and carried it back to the study, noting each door along the hallway was closed.

"Here, help yourself, Francis, I'll be right back."

He scurried back into the kitchen, moving to the back door to check she wasn't outside. Jackson looked up from where he was standing knocking the mud from his boots. "Everythin' alright, Sir?" he asked.

"Have you seen Miss, err, the lady," he asked, remembering at the last moment that Francis could very well overhear, and refrained from using her name.

"Aye. She's asleep, Sir. The poor lass was exhausted. She looks as if she's not slept for a week, which could be right with travelling an' such. She looked downright spooked earlier and ready to pass out when I found her standin' outside. Was there something I can get for ye, Sir?"

Edward was surprised; this was the last thing he had expected of the sassy young woman. He thought she'd have had more stamina that this. And what the hell had spooked her? Surely not his kiss? In hindsight, this was the best outcome he could have hoped for, if she was locked away in her room sleeping, then Francis wouldn't get another chance to ogle her. "Er, yes, if you've finished up out there, maybe you could brew Mr Flecher and me some coffee and bring it to the study?" Jackson nodded and Edward moved back inside and made his way back to his friend.

"That was quick!" Francis said, eyebrows wriggling, I was expecting at least a half hour of entertaining myself. A quickie in the kitchen was it against the stove, you have that flushed look."

"For god's sake, Francis, will you stop already. I've told you, there is nothing like that going on. I was simply rushing around. Miss, er, the maid is feeling under the weather and has retired for the morning, Jackson will bring some coffee through shortly. Now, what delectable treats did I manage to find?" He sat behind his desk, pulling the lid off one of the tins and finding pastries.

"Miss?" Francis hadn't missed that Edward hadn't completed the mystery woman's name.

"Leave it!" Edward growled taking a bite of his pastry.

Francis surprisingly did leave it, and they ate almost in silence. Once their cups and plates were empty, Francis stood and was readying to take his leave, pushing his arms into the long winter-weight coat and wriggling his fingers into his leather gloves, whilst reminding Edward that he would be back two days hence to collect his purchases, when the men were interrupted by a woman's high-pitched voice. "Help me".

Both men spun around, ready to bolt back along the wooden hall, "No," Edward said, "wait for me in my dining room, I'll be back momentarily to see you out," and with that he charged forward towards Abigail's room, knocked once, and upon hearing no sound entered the room and found, nothing. The unmade bed was empty, and he walked quickly around it just in case the woman had fallen, but again there was no one. Where the hell was she? Jackson said she was sleeping. A scream, loud and piercing filled the air, and Edward was once again running.

Chapter Twelve

Mist swirling at her knees, Abigail stepped out tentatively, at this rate she would never reach Mama and Father standing at the edge of the moor where the mist had depleted and where the sun shone down warming them. Abigail was caught in the strange undulating mist, her toes already numb as the ice crystals adhered to her boots and gown, the cold slowly engulfing her body. She had to reach her parents, or she would be frozen, a human statue, never able to escape. "Please Father," she called her arms reaching, "I want to come home, wait for me." Desperate, she took another step and then another, reaching, reaching, she was so close just a few more steps. Something caressed her ankle, and she stilled, what was that? She stepped again, and once more something beneath the mist slid against her; petrified now, she tried to run, but the unseen horror took hold of her legs, trapping, binding, she couldn't shift her feet, but her forward momentum continued and she was falling, tumbling and the mist swirled faster, it was going to devour her and there was nothing she could do. "Help me!" she screamed. The silvery swirl caressed her face, but it felt nothing like the sensual silk she had imagined, it was like leathery fingers stroking, her brow, her cheek, cupping her face and her eyes flew open.

Mr Langley's gentleman caller was touching her, his gloved hand holding her face. Startled, Abigail pushed at him, as she sprang from the seat but as she tried to take a step something pulled tight against her lower legs, and she screamed as she pitched forward to be caught in the man's embrace.

A loud roar sounded from the doorway and Abigail turned her head and through tear-filled eyes watched as Mr Langley prowled toward them. The man who held her, slowly released her from his embrace, simply steadying her instead with a hand to her shoulder as Mr Langley reached them. "She was falling, Edward, all I did was catch her." The man sounded defensive. "She startled and stood, her feet caught the blanket, see?" he swept one arm down to show the crumpled culprit binding her legs.

"And what startled her?" Edward asked, noting that Francis looked guilty as sin. He shook his head in disgust, he knew his friend well enough, he didn't require an answer. "Unhand her," he ordered and pulled Abigail away from his friend, the blanket tightened again, and Abigail's scream startled him. "I mean you no harm, Miss…"

"My leg," she sobbed, and Edward understood immediately.

"Here," he commanded Francis, "hold her shoulders, steady her!" Francis did as he was bid, grabbing Abigail by the arm, totally confused by the conflicting orders. Edward leaned down and so very carefully untangled the rough woollen blanket from her feet and legs before standing and with a quick, "I'll see you in a couple of days, Francis," lifted Abigail, one arm beneath her knees, the other around her back, his hand falling perilously close to her breast. Abigail hooked an arm around his neck and sobbed into his chest as he strode from the room, leaving Francis to watch in bewilderment. Who was that woman that Edward held so protectively? And why was she sleeping in his dining room? As much as he wanted to stay and learn the answers, he'd seen the look on his friend's face, and knew when he wasn't welcome.   Striding from the room, he saw Edward disappearing with the beautiful woman into the storage room along the passage and the plot thickened further, what the hell was going on here? he pondered, as he gained the front door and let himself out.

Edward heard the door bang closed behind Francis and breathed a little easier. He still wanted to know what his friend had done to startle Miss Dumont, and he would ask her just as soon as he'd made her comfortable. He bent and gently placed her on the bed, and upon straightening he stared down at the young woman. Even with the tears streaking her cheeks, she took his breath away and he realized with sudden clarity how Spencer had felt, oh boy, he was in trouble. "Jackson," he called and heard the heavy footfalls come down the hall and stop just inside the door.

"Sir?" the man looked dismayed to find the young lady crying on the bed and his employer standing over her, "what have ye done, Sir?"

Edward looked at him and was about to admonish him, but the look on the older man's face, anguish, disappointment, stopped him dead. He glanced back to the crying woman, and seeing the scene that Jackson saw, blanched and he backed away from the bed a little holding up his hands. "Not what it looks like, old man," he said quickly. "Please, could you bring me a bowl of warm water, and towels." The man's eyes widened further, and Edward could have kicked himself, as he realized what meaning his man had appropriated from his words.

"Jackson, please," Abigail's voice, small and pained came from the bed "Do as he asks." The older man met her gaze across the room. "There is no harm done here, but I need the water quite urgently," she finished on a sob, and Jackson spun to do her bidding.

"Thank you for your assistance, Mr Langley but I'm sure I can take it from here," she moved to sit up straighter and hissed a breath of pain as her skirts shifted, tearing at the wound. "Or maybe not," she squeaked out her voice filled with pain.

Edward looked around for the chair that he'd left by the bed when he'd dragged it in here a few days ago and was surprised to find it behind the door. He pulled it across the room and seated himself near the end of the bed, as he began to slowly gather her gown from the hem and roll it upward closer to where he knew the wound was.

Jackson reappeared in the doorway, stopping short of entering with bowl and towels in hand. "Em, Miss?" he questioned.

"Over here, man.' Edward snapped and pointed to the bottom of the bed, "just put it down there."

Jackson's eyes shot to Abigails, and she nodded her agreement. He strode forward and did what was bid of him and turned and left the room, leaving the door ajar and stepping into the hallway, he spun, put his back to the wall and there he stood, sentry duty, ready to move if the little Miss needed him.

"I'm going to have to soak your gown, Miss Dumont, it's the only way to separate the material from your wound." Edward looked up at her to see a look of agreement on her face and took her silence as acquiescence. He set too, soaking a towel and pressing gently at her gown over and over, the heavy material absorbing the water. Once he was satisfied that the warm water had reached her skin, he began to ease the material away from the angry red blotches. He winced when he could see where the blisters had ruptured. He couldn't look at her face again, unable to bear watching the pain that flittered across her beautiful features, knowing if he saw, he wouldn't be able to continue being the cause of such discomfort. To distract her, he asked. "What was it that startled you from your slumber, Miss Dumont?"

Abigail shuddered, partly due to the cold room, but more so at the memory of her nightmare. "I was dreaming, Mr Langley, and not a pleasant dream. I was outside and something hidden in the mist held my ankles bound, I pitched forward, falling into the grey swirl and something leathery held my face, stroking and I opened my eyes to find your friend's gloved hand on my skin. I was startled, jumped up and I screamed as I fell."

Edward's jaw clenched. How dare Francis put his hands on his woman. Frightening her! Wait, had he just thought 'his woman?' She wasn't his, he couldn't have her, she still belonged to Spencer. He looked to her pale face and the realization sunk in, he may not be able to have her, but by God, he wanted her.

With her wound cleansed, he stood shakily and with a slight bow said, "I'm sorry. He shouldn't have startled you awake like that."   But as he searched her face, her eyes swimming in tears, he couldn't help but wonder, if it had been him that woke her, would she have startled so? "Err, I'll leave you now, but I'll send Jackson with some gauze and bandages." He saw her nod, her body shivering, the room was cold, and her gown drenched about her legs; without a word, he wrapped the blanket around her and strode to the door.

"Thank you," Abigail said as he closed her door.

Abigail was freezing. She snuggled herself into the blanket the best she could, and drawing her gown above her knees, she managed to slip her uninjured leg beneath the covers, leaving only her injured leg open to the cold as her wound still wept. Sitting back, she laid her head on the wall and waited for the bandages to arrive.

Chapter Thirteen

Edward stepped from Miss Dumont's room straight into an ambush, there was no other word for it. As soon as her door was closed, Jackson stood to attention, and said "A word with ye, Sir." One look at Jackson's lined old face with his wind-reddened cheeks, wide eyes and flaring nostrils, Edward knew he was about to get a tongue lashing. Yes, Jackson was an employee, but he was so much more. He had been Stable Manager to Edward's father's for as long as Edward could remember. Jackson that taught him to ride as a young boy, and it was Jackson that stood by his side, offering his strength to a distraught Edward at his father graveside. And now, his most trusted employee and father figure was angry, and probably for good reason.

As soon as the study door clicked shut, Jackson snapped, "What're yer intentions toward Miss Dumont?"

"No intent at all," Edward answered, although he found he couldn't look the older man in the eye. "She is simply here to help with the chores."

Jackson shook his head. "Don't ye lie to me, lad. We never get anyone in to help over the holiday time. Ye've sent the staff off every year, just like yer father did, so why is she here?"

"Miss Dumont is a rumourmonger and a tease, who needs to be taught a lesson in humility." Edward looked him in the eye now, speaking his truth.

"And ye think scaring the lass, housing her in a storage room which ye wouldn't sleep a dog in is the right way about it? When I knocked on her door this mornin', I was met with a lass that hadn't slept a wink, wearing a torn dress, with her outdoor wear slung around her shoulders shivering with cold. I'm disappointed in ye, boy."

Edward flinched, feeling like a young lad again and being told off for taking a switch to his horse; Jackson had admonished him for using pain to make his horse do his bidding, and now, now he had disappointed him again by using cruelty to avenge his cousin's damaged reputation. He'd known that room was near freezing, worse at this time of the year, but he'd wanted her to be miserable. He'd cleared and readied the storage room himself whilst his anger rode him, controlling him. He wasn't normally this person, so what the hell was he doing?

Sighing deeply, he tried to explain. "I had a plan, Jackson, it just wasn't a well thought out one. Spencer has been the victim of a serpent's tongue, and that tongue belongs, I believe, to Miss Dumont. Spencer asked my assistance, and I could not refuse."

"And what was it that young Mr Ashcroft asked of ye exactly?" he asked gruffly.

"Well, he asked, um, he wanted me to... I, well he," Edward closed his eyes, trying to think and then sighed, "he never actually got around to asking me to do anything. I was furious when he told me he'd been victimized, bullied by a bunch of gossip mongers and ..."

"And ye decided all on yer own to bully the woman in return?" Jackson finished for him, shaking his head. "And how's that workin' for ye? he asked. "There's an injured lady, staying with no chaperone in yer home, with two males in attendance and a third whose witness to that fact. I'm not sure that was what yer cousin had in mind, do ye?"

Edward moved behind his desk and sat heavily, elbows resting on the large blotter pad and dropped his head into his hands, eyes staring at the blue smear, where Francis had negligently dropped his pen. Francis wouldn't say anything about the woman he'd caught his friend kissing, would he? Who was he kidding, it was Francis, he couldn't ever keep a secret. And now Edward had managed to stir the man's curiosity by being so mysterious; He'd inadvertently made this a game for his long-time acquaintance.

"Oh, Jackson, you don't know the half of it, Francis didn't just see Miss Dumont, he walked in on me kissing her. What do I do now?"

"First, we're going to move Miss Dumont from the storage room. I'll light the fire and organise a tray for the front guest room while ye take her those bandages. I'll be in shortly to collect her trunk. Once she is taken care of, yer going to tell me the whole story and then see what's to be done."

<u>**Chapter Fourteen**</u>

Abigail could not get warm. No matter how she arranged the blankets, the room was just too cold. Her fingers were numb, and she was pretty sure, if there had been a mirror in her room, it would show her as pale faced and blue lipped. Her jaw ached from her teeth constantly chattering. All the bravado she'd felt in Mr Langley's study only that morning, was long gone. She was miserable. She was trapped and all she longed for was to be warm and cosy in her own bed, in her own room.

When the gentle knock sounded at the door, she answered quickly, hoping that Jackson had finally brought her the bandages so she could wrap her wound and then finally, she could get out of this wet gown. She hadn't seen the point in trying to change it, until the weeping blisters were covered, or she'd wind up back in the same predicament. "Come in, Jackson."

Her eyes widened when the door swung open and instead of the kindly face of the old man, there stood Mr Langley.

"Miss Dumont, pardon the intrusion, but I've brought you the gauze and bandages. Can you manage on your own, or would you perhaps permit me to assist?"

"I thank you, Mr Langley, but I fear I've taken more than enough of your time. If you'd kindly leave them on the chair."

Edward stood for a long moment, then moved across to the chair and deposited the goods. His breath came out in cloudy puffs, in the cold room and he dithered another moment or two as if trying to find words to say; but finally gave in and nodding in her direction, he left the room, closing the door behind him.

Once the door snibbed shut, she threw the blanket off. Moving stiffly, she took hold of the gauze, placing it against the raw skin of her burn and wrapped the bandage round and round, firm enough to hold the gauze in place and securing it with the pin.   She stood gingerly, checking that nothing pulled at the tender skin as she moved her leg. Once satisfied, she opened her trunk and pulled her third gown from where it was folded. At this rate, she'd be running out of clean clothes, first gown damaged by the fire and Mr Langley shredding it, the second drenched and with no heating in her room, she wondered how she would manage to dry it. As quickly as her frozen fingers would allow, she unbuttoned her bodice and slipped it from her shoulders, oh God, it was so cold, her skin was covered in gooseflesh as she hurried to push her feet through the skirts and pull the new gown up over her hips and shrugging it over her shoulders before buttoning herself in.   Just in time. A knock came at the door, and she bid a breathless, "come in."

If she was expecting Mr Langley again, she would be disappointed, as Jackson appeared in the door frame.

"I've come to collect yer trunk, Miss. And if ye'd care to carry the smaller bag, I'll take ye to yer new quarters."

Abigail was shocked! "What, I mean, where?"

"If ye'll just follow me, Miss." And with that said, he hefted the heavy trunk and backed his way out of the room and headed toward the staircase. Abigail quickly gathered the minimal items that she'd unpacked, and draping the wet gown over her arm and leaving the ruined one lying on the floor, she lifted the bag and left the cold room without a second glance. She followed Jackson up the dark wooded stairs to the second floor. As she scurried along the polished floorboards, she was stunned at the opulence of the rooms she glanced in as she hurried past. She paused in the doorway where Jackson had disappeared and simply stood, eyes wide as she took in her new quarters. "Come on in, Miss, I'll leave ye to unpack." He sidled past her and out into the hallway, pulling the door too behind him.

She moved further into the room, taking in the luxury before her. Who would have thought it, this room was beautiful. Dropping her belongings on the floor, she climbed and dropped herself onto the large feather quilt, the mattress was comfortable, neither too hard, nor too soft and as she spread her arms out, she realized she couldn't reach both sides at the same time, the bed was huge. Rolling to her stomach, the headboard caught her eye, and she reached a hand to caress the intricate carvings of flowers and birds, noting the four posts were similarly carved, she'd never seen the likes.

Climbing from the bed, and moving to the fireplace, she held her cold hands to the flames and delighted in the tiny pin pricks of heat that rushed across her fingertips, the comfortable high backed chair seemed to beckon and she moved to sit on its plush cushion, her legs straight, reaching toward the blazing logs, wriggling her toes at the blissful heat. The room was carpeted with a large cream rug that held the centre of the room and from where she sat, she could see a dressing table complete with mirror. She stood and moved toward it then gasped in dismay at the sight that was reflected. She looked like a ragamuffin, a street urchin, her hair, that she'd pinned, now lay in a knotted mess about her shoulders, and pale skin, showed starkly the dark puffiness below her eyes.   No wonder Mr Langley's gentleman friend had believed her to be a maid.

With shaking fingers, she pulled the rest of the pins from her hair and retrieving her brush, stroked the long auburn tresses, teasing out the tangled knots before twisting and securing it back atop her head.

She could scarce believe the difference in her circumstance, a freezing, barely furnished room to the warmth and luxury of her new surroundings. Maybe she should have been more aggressive in her manner when she first arrived, for it seemed her speech to Mr Langley that morning had changed his mind about keeping her housed in the servants' quarters.

Moving to the window, she drew the heavy drapery across the runners and stood looking at the vista before her. It was mesmerising! What had she been so frightened of? The mist, as Jackson had said, had evaporated and the sun cast a golden glow across the land. It really was beautiful and for the first time since arriving, Abigail found she was content.

<u>**Chapter Fifteen**</u>

Edward wasn't fairing quite as well as the young lady upstairs!

Jackson had returned as promised and was now seated waiting for an explanation, as to why Miss Dumont came to be victim to such beastly behaviour, whilst Edward paced about the room.

"Start at the beginning, Sir, I find that's a good place to begin a story. Where did ye meet, Miss Dumont?

"I met Miss Dumont when you dropped her off at the front door." The older man looked at him incredulously.

"Ye'd never met the lass? Then why…"

"Spencer." Edward finally said. "Spencer is in love with Miss Dumont. They were meant to wed. But events, I cannot speak of, got out of hand and Miss Dumont refused to receive him, and then there were the rumours. Only three people knew what happened, Spencer, Lord Dandion, who both have been attacked by the lies, and Miss Dumont, therefore it is only logical to surmise the rumours must have started with her."

"Well, rumours are a nasty thing. Ye say Mr Ashcroft is in love with the lady? So, tell me, why were ye kissing her?"

"I, um," Edward rolled his eyes, this was going to be harder to explain, he couldn't just say he lost control of himself. Even if it was the truth. "She was giving me a piece of her mind and I, err, thought it was the quickest way to shut her up. I didn't think, Jackson. Come on man, have you never done anything on impulse?"

"Aye, I have, but never with another man's woman. I asked ye before what yer intentions for this young miss, and now I'm askin' ye again. Do ye have feelings for Miss Dumont?"

Edward sat and just as quickly stood again and resumed his pacing. How to answer a question he'd been tormenting himself with. There was just something about the woman, that called to him, excited him like no other had and knowing she belonged to his cousin, well, he was envious, jealous and so very frustrated that he'd not met her first. She was promised to Spencer and yet, Edward wanted her. She should belong to him.

When she hadn't pulled free of his embrace as he'd plundered her mouth, he could still taste her on his lips, oh those so soft lips. Spencer had been right; one kiss was not enough. But it wasn't just the kiss, he wondered at his intense reaction when she had screamed, the anger that fuelled him when discovering Fletcher with his hands on her. Hell, he'd wanted to rip the man limb from limb. And then he'd swung her into his arms like a bloody caveman, a desperate bid to get her as far from the other man as quickly as he could. The action screamed MINE, and that was a thought he shouldn't have allowed himself while she'd pressed her tear-stained cheek against his chest, and wrapped her arms around his neck, a thought he could never voice, because she wasn't his.

"I've never met anyone like her," he finally answered. "My plan was to teach her a lesson in humility, make her re-think what she could be throwing away by hurting Spencer. It was to be you and me, nobody was meant to know she was here, it was so simple. She'd pay her debt for hurting Spence and then I'd return her home, no harm, no foul. Francis was never meant to see her, and I certainly never intended to..." he left the rest unsaid, but the look on his face spoke volumes. He was falling in love with Miss Dumont!

Jackson stood and walked to where Edward had stopped his pacing and now stared unseeingly out of the window. "Do you have proof that she's the rumourmonger? Did Mr Ashcroft say so?"

Edward sighed, "No, not specifically, but Spencer told me that there had been no other witnesses."

"No other witnesses that he knows of," Jackson mused, then seeing the horrified look on Edward's face he added, "I'm sure it'll be alright, Sir. Whilst ye work out those feelings, I suggest Miss Dumont continue to assist around the house, to pay back her father's debt, but ye need to refrain from being rude and treating her as ye are, she is a lady, and needs to be treated as such, at least until ye have proof that she is the guilty party."

Edward grimaced, "That's the other thing. The debt isn't real. It doesn't exist. I fabricated the story to get my hands on Miss Dumont. Her father wasn't at the card table when I came across him at the club, but he was 'in his cups', and with a little assistance I increased his inebriated state. I had him sign the wager, which I then followed up the next morning when I visited his home and told him I would take the payment in the form of his daughter."

"Ye mean, he owed you nought, and you still collected. What has gotten into ye, lad?" Jackson growled.

"I know, Jackson, I wasn't thinking straight , I was angry, and then I had a drink and, and now I don't know how to set right all my wrongs. Miss Dumont is nothing like I'd imagined. She's doesn't appear to be a heartless woman set to ruin a man, and the little time I've spent with her, well, I'd be surprised if she'd ever say a bad word about anyone, well except maybe me.   And now, when she leaves here, she will assuredly fall back into Spencer's arms as I originally planned, except ..."

"Except what?" Jackson probed.

"Except, that is not where I want her to be, I want her in my arms!"

Chapter Sixteen

Abigail descended the staircase marvelling at her change of circumstance. She was happy to fulfil the payment of the debt, now that she was warm and had comfortable accommodation. She was no longer looking at the house as a prison, and Mr Langley her jailer. Instead, she found herself looking forward to seeing the enigmatic man. She no longer feared him, quite the opposite in fact. Twice now, she'd been in his arms. The first embrace and his kiss, surprised her, but was not, she realized after much deliberation, unwelcome. And the second instance he held her in his arms, there was no ardour, but the closeness, the safety she felt as he'd carried her to her cot, the gentleness of his movements, his hard stare intense when it met her own.

She could hear muffled voices coming from the study, and crept silently passed, continuing toward the kitchen, where she began preparations for the evening meal. The afternoon was quickly closing in, the weak sun once again hidden behind heavy cloud and the heavy pitter patter of rain beat a rhythm on the window. Needing more light, she took a candle, setting it aflame and went along the hallway, holding it to the wick of the light sconces before moving to the dining room to bring a bright yellow glow to the room. Why Mr Langley hadn't used the sconces last evening was beyond her, it would have made her introduction to the house so much friendlier. Although, there had been nothing polite or friendly about him. It seemed almost, she realized, as if he disliked her. But why? She had never met the man.

She stoked the fire, to keep the room toasty warm, as the wind picked up outside, the rain pelted the windows the sound like tiny pebbles thrown against glass, making her shiver and thankful that the house was a sturdy build. Back in the kitchen she proceeded to strain the vegetables and added them to the large slices of chicken pie she'd plated for the three of them. Leaving her own and Jackson's meal on the small wooden table she took Mr Langley's into his dining room.

Setting his meal on the table, she moved to the still closed study door and knocked, waiting patiently for a response, and when none came, she leaned in lifted her hand to rap a little harder when the door was flung wide, and her knuckled hand struck a hard, broad chest instead.

Mr Langley covered her hand, his long fingers capturing hers, his other braced her shoulder to stop her stumbling forward.

Slightly breathless, the crawling tickle of embarrassment inching its way up her neck to her face, she made to pull her hand back, but the fingers holding hers, didn't immediately release and she stilled, her body reacting pleasantly to his touch, combined with the feel of him beneath her fingertips. She gulped and stuttered out. "D-d-dinner is served, Mr Langley."

"Thank you, Miss Dumont," he responded, and then to her surprise, he moved her hand from his chest, placed it on his forearm and led her back toward the dining room. "Please, join me." It wasn't a question she realised and once he released her arm, she moved back to the kitchen to collect her plate, bringing it to the dining room and placed it to the right of him, then settled herself stiffly into her seat, and picked up her knife and fork. Once she'd taken her first bite, Mr Langley followed suit, with ne'er a word spoken, they ate in companionable silence.

Mr Langley rose and poured wine, a rich red, into two glasses, passing her one, as he sat back, one hand across his stomach, and sipped as he studied her. "That was a fine meal, Miss Dumont." She acknowledged the compliment with a slight nod and a flash of a smile. His eyes widened, and his breath left him in a rush. It felt like the room was lit by a bolt of lightning, the strike a direct hit to his chest. Her smile, little as it had been changed her features. She was beautiful with the slight tilt to her lips and flash of white teeth, but when she smiled, she was magnificent, and he knew he must make her do it again and again. But first, he had to make amends. "I feel, I need to apologise for my behaviour upon your arrival last night."

Abigail regarded him, her green gaze sparkling in the light of the flickering lamp, she took a delicate sip from her glass as he waited for her to accept his apology.

"Mr Langley," She went quiet again, taking a moment to gather her thoughts and courage. "Why did you kiss me?"

<u>Chapter Seventeen</u>

Edward's eyebrows shot up, then scrunched into a hard frown. He'd not been expecting that.

He'd assumed she would have questions, for which he had makeshift answers at the ready. *How long was she to stay? Was the debt complete upon her leaving? How was her working here reimbursing his purse?* Instead, she'd blindsided him! This was not one of the questions he'd been practising to answer with Jackson that afternoon.

'Why had he kissed her?'

Why indeed. To shut her up, to stop the rant, partly he supposed. But truthfully, he couldn't have stopped himself, even if he had wanted to. She had been a thing of pure beauty; intelligent, forceful, argumentative, her eyes had flashed in anger and defiance, her mouth sprouting words that nobody had ever dared utter to his face, and with the aggressiveness of her tirade, her chest rose and fell as she breathed fast and heavy. There was no thought. He wanted to touch her, to hold her, and caress her lips into silence with his own.

She was still looking at him, waiting in silence for his answer. What to say? Maybe a part truth would suffice. "I was mesmerised, Miss Dumont. Your attack surprised and, in all honesty, delighted me. I heard words which should have infuriated me, but coming from between such sweet lips, I discovered anger wasn't the controlling force in which to fight the battle you presented. Desire was! The desire to feel the movement of your lips with my own, I needed to taste your words, to assess if they were angry ones or merely argumentative. My father, God rest his soul, would often say that 'anger tasted bitter on the tongue,' and I felt in that moment, I must test his words. And let me assure you Miss Dumont, the taste of your tongue, was not bitter, YOU were NOT angry."

Abigail startled; was it not anger then that had her raising her voice to him that very morning? No, she thought, not anger, something else. Something that evaporated as his lips had caressed hers, and his tongue plundered. It had been despair. Despair that had swiftly turned to desire as she kissed him back.

"You, my lady did not taste bitter,' he continued. "You were sweet like honey, and just like the honey maker, when attacked, you countered with a sting, a venomous sting of words. But your flavour, was heady, and I found I wanted more, but alas we were interrupted, and I was left craving ..."

Edward moved as he spoke, his fingers gently pulling the wine glass from her hand to deposit it on the table, his eyes fixed on hers, mesmerised by the depth of those deep green pools. "... another ... delicious ... taste." And his lips came to rest once more against hers. His tongue gently probing, searching for entry, she sighed as she sank into him, her lips parted and he pushed home, lost in the succulent sweet-honeyed warmth, imbued with the rich aroma of wine.

His mouth sipped at her delicate lips, his tongue caressed hers gently, insistently. His hands roved, shimmying from her waist up her arms, along her shoulders, halting only when they reached the slender column of her neck, and her soft, warm flesh. His thumb stroked along her pulse point, feeling the thrum of her heartbeat, fast, fluttery like a trapped bird. Pulling his lips from hers, his face hovered so very close, breathing her in. "Oh, Miss Dumont, your lips are seductive, one taste, that was never going to be enough." He almost groaned as she leant forward closing the breach and once again, he was kissing her, and yet… his words were like a trigger, he'd heard something very similar. His brain searched and he got his answer, and he reared back.

Spencer!

Chapter Eighteen

Abigail looked stricken as Mr Langley moved swiftly away, he paced across the room stopping before the hearth and staring down into the flickering, orange flames.

She did not move. She couldn't! Frozen in place, the only movement was that of her erratic heartbeat which she was certain was about to tear its way from beneath her skin. Her breath came in heavy pants making her head spin a little. But what affected her most was the loss of his hands on her skin, his lips on hers. What had she done wrong? Why had he stopped?

Time ticked by and he didn't turn, didn't say a word. An embarrassed flush scorched her already heated cheeks, what must he think of her, that she would give herself so freely. Why, she hardly knew what to think of herself. She rose on shaking legs and without another look in his direction, she began to gather the plates, piling the dirty dishes onto the tray, she felt his eyes then, watching her every move; but she refused to turn and face him, she pulled her shoulders back and strode from the room, hastily making her way back to the kitchen. She kicked the heavy door closed and then depositing the tray on the work bench, moved to the sink and splashed cold water over her burning cheeks. She was mortified, humiliated at her wanton behaviour.

He was playing with her. Making her want him, only for him to turn away, leaving her confused, frustrated. It seemed he was not above taking advantage of her situation. Taking liberties, that... No, no, no she must be honest with herself. He hadn't taken liberties; in fact, he'd bestowed on her a kiss, a caress, he'd given her everything her heart had yearned but had never believed she'd find. How could her feelings run so deep for a man she barely knew?   And what would become of those feelings once the debt had been paid, and he sent her away?

Her nervous hands moved of their own volition, washing, drying and packing dishes as though she'd been doing this kind of labour forever, and yet when she finally put the last of the plates on the shelf, she found she couldn't remember having washed any of them, her head so filled with Mr Langley.

All she wanted was to hide, take to her bed chamber and bury her shame beneath the blankets. She peered around the kitchen door, and then soundlessly made her way along the hallway and gingerly climbed the staircase, holding her breath as her foot caught a squeaky board, and releasing it once she gained the top of the stairs, taking a quick peak over the banister to assure herself she'd not been observed, before opening her door and slipping inside; she closed it softly behind her.

Abigail slept fitfully. Each time her eyes closed, she dreamt of Mr Langley's hands and lips caressing her body as she writhed beneath his ministrations. Only to awaken without him, her body hot and aching for his touch. Finally, she gave up trying to sleep at all, instead slipping from the bed and taking the heavy feather-filled cover she curled into a chair beside the window and watched as the storm outside lit the countryside and listened as thunder boomed out its torment in a voice that rattled the glass. The rain, tears on the window reflecting those on her cheeks as Abigail realized her feelings would lead to nought and she would be delivered home to live a life without Mr Langley.

She must keep her distance, do her work and hide in her room whenever possible. It was the only way to curb her growing feelings.

Chapter Nineteen

Edward slumped over his desk. The empty bottle lay broken on the floor, where he'd dropped it when the thunder had startled him; he paid it no heed. Quite frankly, the bottle meant nothing to him now that it was empty. He groaned, lifting his head as the door swung open and Jackson stood in a pool of light, surveying the scene of Edwards pity party. Jackson shook his head and moved toward Edward, watching as the man's eyes narrowed to slits the closer the light got to him. Jackson set the lamp on the floor and began collecting the sharp-edged pieces of glass and placing them on the blackened brick of the hearth before returning to Edward. "Come on, lad," he said, easing his arm around his shoulders and hefting the large man to his feet. "Let's get you to bed."

"I done," Edward hiccupped, "did it."

'Did what?" Jackson asked as he manoeuvred Edward out of the door and toward the stairs.

"Kished Mish Dumon, mmm she tasse wine," he slurred, "love Mish Dumon."

Jackson man-handled him to his room and removed his shoes, pulling the blankets up and handing him the chamber from beneath the bed, "Ye'd best be sleeping with this close by, lad." He said, before moving to sit in the chair before the fire. He'd seen the young man through many nights such as this after his father had passed, and again after he'd sustained his injury, as the alcohol he imbibed had numbed that pain as well.

As the storm outside finally blew itself out, Edward emptied the last of his stomach contents and Jackson took the pot, leaving the room and closing the door. He knew the lad would sleep now and be right as rain when he woke. The old man emptied the pot, then collected and disposed of the glass shards from the study before finally crawling into his own bed to ponder Edwards words and maybe get a quick nap in before he had to get up and check for storm damage and to see to the horses.

Edward woke with a clear head, a foul taste in his mouth and a numb heart. What was he to do? Miss Dumont belonged to his cousin; he couldn't break Spencer's heart by stealing away his bride. But if he didn't, then his own heart would be left empty. His not so cleverly devised plan had backfired the moment he set eyes on the gorgeous woman stepping from the carriage. No, truth be told, it had been from the moment he'd seen her peek through the wooden balusters, as she'd spied from the staircase. His anger had taken a side-step and he'd been swamped with feelings he'd never expected.

His plan was never going to work. Miss Dumont had taken to the mundane maids' tasks with very little effort, even seeming to enjoy creating the tasty meals she served up. She was a surprise, so much intrigue in one little package. Warm, kind and caring to all walks of life it seemed, he hadn't failed to see the way she interacted with Jackson; she was belligerent, aggressive to be sure when angered, her quick mind sharpened her tongue and yet, she spoke only her truth. She'd put him down quickly, efficiently, truthfully; so much so he'd had to stop her with a much more pleasant use of that tantalising mouth. And yet, he realized, during their short time together, not once had she done anything to make him believe she was capable of such cruelty as to inflict such pain with vindictive gossip.

He could scarce believe it of her, but what other option was there? She was the only party involved, which could garner enough sympathy to be left without stain on her character. He knew without doubt that his cousin was innocent, and Lord Dandion would most assuredly not be besmirching his own name. Yes, it was commonly *thought* that he may '*prefer*' male company, and most definitely *known* by a handful of likeminded gentlemen, but it was certainly not open for discussion. Which left, Miss Dumont.

He decided he would spend a little time getting to know her better. No kissing, no feelings, just to decide if she had a darker side to her character.

A sound at his door had him striding to open it, and he watched as Jackson brought in hot water for his wash.

"Feeling better today, Sir." He asked as he put the basin down.

"I am sorry, Jackson. I may have had a bit too much to drink last night, my mouth feels like ashes," he replied.

Jackson cocked his head and gave a grin. "Ay, ye were well in ye cups when I hauled ye to yer room." He saw Edward swing around to stare at him, as he continued "so ye obviously like kissing the young Miss," he teased.

Edward hung his head, "Damn, what else did I say?" he growled.

"Not a lot, and with the way ye was slurrin' I doubt much would be understood anyhow." Jackson answered before heading to the door, "Oh, except of course that ye love Mish Dumon." Jackson chuckled and left the room, closing the door on Edward's shocked expression.

His breakfast was a lonely affair. Miss Dumont had arranged his meal at his usual place setting and as he sat with his coffee, his eyes were drawn time and again to the empty seat where she'd joined him last evening. His mind on the ardent kisses they'd shared, and he was certain they were shared, there had been no hesitancy on her behalf, and she appeared to enjoy his touch. Did this mean that she was over her relationship with his cousin? Or had she not shared Spencer's feelings at all? No, no he could not see her toying with a man's feelings, especially once their intentions were made clear. And yet, she was kissing him, and he'd certainly not made any declaration toward her, in fact he'd done the exact opposite when she'd come at him with that ridiculous marriage insinuation of her fathers. Oh, she was a conundrum with her beautiful face and spectacular eyes that told so many stories, her face an open book for anyone to read, if one could only read the foreign tongue in which it was printed.

Yes, he must most definitely spend more time with her, get to know her. Only then could he decide if she were indeed predisposed of deception.

<u>**Chapter Twenty**</u>

Abigail had risen early from the chair in which she'd nodded through the night. Crept downstairs and had used the bellows to pump the few embers in the fire grate back to life. Breakfast was prepared and the spread placed in the dining room and now she sat at the table in the kitchen, her own meal of sticky porridge before her. She was wondering how Bessie had managed to make her oatmeal so creamy and lump free, she must ask her beloved friend when she returned home. That thought soured even the sweet, dark molasses she'd drizzled on her breakfast, and she swallowed quickly. She didn't want to leave here, 'no, be honest' she told herself; she didn't want to leave him!

Jackson appeared at the doorway, "Mornin', Miss," his voice rumbled as he combed his wet, receding hair away from his face with long, gnarled fingers. "Did ye sleep well? Or did the storm keep ye awake?"

"I slept fitfully indeed. Though the storm was a fine sight to behold, and I sat much of the night beside the window taking in the sights of the moor lit by lightning."

"Aye, tiz a sight alreet." He helped himself from the pot on the stove and sat heavily in the chair opposite and took a large spoonful of the thick porridge and swallowed with what appeared to be delight, "Ah, that hits the spot. Warms the cockles, don' it?" he grinned and shovelled in another mouthful. Abigail smiled, relieved that he was enjoying the thick, slightly lumpy mush.

"Jackson, may I ask you a question about Mr Langley?"

"Certainly, Miss and if I can I'll answer."

"Why does he not stay in town for the winter, like so many of the other gentlemen?" she asked and added, "Cornwall is rather a long journey to make to enjoy the company of his peers."

"Ah yes, a long way indeed. The master spent many a winter in town enjoying all that society offers until his father passed away and then he himself was injured. He rarely visits now, content on running his business from home."

"I'm sorry for the loss of his father, I presume he was close."

"Aye, he was. The Mistress, his mother died when he was just a young 'un, and his father raised 'im alone, and made a fine young man of 'im."

"Hmm," she said side-eying him, which spoke volumes of how well she thought he may have been brought up; thinking about how she came to be here and questioning the 'fine young man' comment. "You mentioned an injury; you mean his scar? What…"

"No, Miss, not my story to tell, ye want to know, ye can ask 'im yerself. I've probably said too much as tiz." He gave her a nod and a "thank ye kindly for the porridge." And he stood and made his way from the room.

Abigail slowly cleared her bowl away then let out a shriek when the door flew open, banging against the wall.

"I'm dreadfully sorry, Miss Dumont, I didn't mean to give you a fright. Erm, thank you for my meal, it was delicious as always."

"You're very welcome, Sir," she responded breathlessly.

"I was wondering, Miss Dumont. Do you ride?"

"I do indeed, Sir, my father taught me when I was but a child."

"Well, would you do me the honour of taking a ride with me this morning? The sun is just up, and the mist won't make an appearance today, thanks to last night's storm."

Abigail bit her lip, she was sorely tempted by the offer. A good ride to blow away the cobwebs from the last few days sounded blissful, but it wouldn't be conducive to her need to keep her distance from Mr Langley. She hoped he couldn't read the longing in her eyes as she came up with an excuse. "Thank you, that would have been most pleasant, alas, I did not pack my riding habit."

She ducked her head and made to move past him, "I'll go and clear your breakfast table."

"Wait!" she stopped and looked up at him, she was far to close and his body, his very presence towering over her, made her long to lean in closer, feel the heat from his body. "I pre-empted your response and have found you a suitable habit, I'm quite sure it will fit, my mother was a similar build."

"I...err," Abigail was at a loss for words.

"I know it's not the kind of habit that you'd be used to, but I promise, it is clean and well kept. My father saw to it that all my mother's items were stored, and they've just been waiting for someone to have a need of them. Please, Miss Dumont, do say, yes!"

How could she refuse? She longed for a ride. She could do this, she could go riding and keep her distance from the man, lock away her feelings and protect her heart.

"I would love to," she agreed smiling widely.

"Good, good," Edward managed, enjoying the sight of the smile that lit the room. "I'll deliver it to your room and await you in my study; shall we say a half hour?"

Abigail gave a nod, and departed the kitchen, her skirts brushing Mr Langley as she passed. She cleared his plate and tidied away in record time. Then headed to her room with a little skip to her step.

She gazed at her reflection, twisting this way and that admiring how the ankle length skirt enhanced her tiny waist and flared across the hips. The collar on the white linen shirt stood stiffly, emphasizing the long, slender column of her neck and when she completed the outfit with the jacket, of matching tweed to the skirt, it's collar also rose to just below her ears. It was adorned with ornate buttons, which seemed to take most of the allotted half an hour to fasten. The outfit in its entirety gave her a delightfully flattering hourglass shape and as she primped and preened, she couldn't help but wonder how well Mr Langley would like this look on her.

As she descended the staircase, she almost held her breath when Mr Langley stepped from his study and regarded her with a heated look, which was there and gone so fast she wondered if she were seeing things. His face was passive as he reached for her hand at the final step and assisted her toward the front door. "If I may be so bold, Miss Dumont, to compliment you, on how perfectly wonderful you look."

"Thank you, Sir. Your mother had very good taste, I feel anyone would look well dressed in such a fine garment." She allowed him to settle her heavy coat about her shoulders and pass her gloves. "Is it so very cold outside that I'll need two coats?"

"The sun may be shining, Miss Dumont, but do not be fooled into thinking that just because the sun is out that it will be warm, believe me, it will be damned cold out." He shrugged into his own woollen coat and pulled on his leather riding gloves. Then proceeded to lead her outside to where Jackson was standing holding two beautiful beasts.

Chapter Twenty-One

Edward assisted Miss Dumont into her saddle, then held the stirrup as she slipped her left foot into it and talked soothingly to the horse to keep her steady as Abigail lifted her right knee to settle around the top pommel and adjusted her skirts before taking the reins from him, smiling her gratitude. He gave a nod acknowledging her thanks and quickly mounted his own horse and with a wave to Jackson, he moved away, with Miss Dumont beside him. He found he had great difficulty keeping his eyes forward, the woman sat her horse magnificently, her posture superb and he felt he must compliment her yet again.

"Miss Dumont, you must have been a fine student, you sit your mount perfectly."

"I thank you, Sir. Anyone would look good on such a fine mare; she is a beautiful animal." He noted how with each compliment given, she managed to steer it away from herself; the habit, now the mare, could she not take a compliment for herself, he wondered.

"She is indeed, and a very gentle mount. She now belongs to Mr Fletcher; she is one of the two horses he purchased on his visit."

Abigail turned away to hide the instant flush to her cheeks at the mention of the man who'd intruded on such a private moment.

Edward could have kicked himself, why had he bought up Francis? "Miss Dumont, please, I feel I must apologise for my behaviour, and also that of my friend, he was not expected at the house, but even so, he was most invasive coming into my study as he did and to not back away again once he came upon us was terribly ill-mannered of him."

"Mr Langley, do you realize that you spend much of your time apologising to me?" she jested. "Mayhap you should not do things which require an apology," she teased. "And I could not blame you for the ill-breeding of your friend, and thus you should not feel the need to apologise on his behalf."

"Then I shall take it all back," he laughed, and she joined in the good humour as they rode on, the horses carefully placing their feet on the hard frosted ground.

It was truly a delightful day. The sun shone brightly, though only in a pretence to warm the earth, as its strong rays, as Edward said, only brightened the day, they were not strong enough to stave off the frigid winds or remove the bite from the frosty air which made one's chest ache upon inhaling.

"Your fam..." Edward started and at the same time, Abigail said

"I asked Jack.." they both closed their mouths.

"Please, go on," Edward said finally.

"I was asking Jackson why you don't visit town," she said.

"And what did he answer?" he frowned at her.

"He said you seemed to prefer to stay closer to home and run your business. He did admit that you were once a reveller, quite happy in high society."

His frown disappeared and he grinned, and her heart beat double time. Oh, how very handsome he was.

"Yes, indeed. I enjoyed a good party. Maybe a little too much enjoyment on occasion. And then my father passed away and I came home to take care of the business. The stables had been his life, you see." He stopped talking and seemed to drift away on his thoughts.

"I'm sorry for your loss," she said, and was rewarded with a small smile.

"Thank you, Miss Dumont. It was a few years back now, but I do still miss him."

"Mr Langley, may I ask a personal question?" she asked.

"You can ask anything, whether I answer, well that remains to be seen," he replied.

"Jackson also said something about you staying away from town because of your accident, but when I enquired, he said it was not for him to tell. Are you inclined to tell me your story?"

Edwards hand lifted and his fingers drew down the line marking his face. "Tiz partly the reason I don't visit town; people are cruel with their stares and comments. It was no accident though. A knife did this," he said slowly, watching her reaction, her face changed from interested to shock. "A horse thief thought he could take me on and steal the horses that Jackson and I were delivering to a client. We each had two horses on lead, Jackson was behind a little way and the assailant obviously didn't realize I wasn't alone. I didn't see the attack coming, like some kind of creature he jumped at me from the branches I was riding under, landed in front of me on my saddle, his knife at the ready to cut my throat, luckily my horse reared, spooked I suppose by the sudden extra weight, this hero here," he leant and patted the neck of his horse, "he saved my life. The man had been mid-swipe, knife aimed at my throat, instead, his arm flew upward, his knife slicing my face instead. We were both thrown to the ground, his knife lost, and we fought, I managed to pin him as Jackson appeared."

"Oh, my. What happened to him?" she asked breathlessly.

"He was brought to the magistrate and tried. And I was left with his calling card for all to read," he said, voice flat, but his eyes sparked with anger.

So lost in his story of horror, both failed to notice the small creature startled from its hiding place, until Abigail's horse whinnied loudly, her legs dancing as a weasel, streaked between the startled animal's feet and disappeared beneath a patch of heather. Abigail held tight, trying to quiet the spooked animal, but alas, it was too late, the horse leapt forward breaking into a gallop and all Abigail could do was hang on, trying to remain seated. She heard a guttural yell which she barely registered, all sounds drowned by the rushing blood in her veins; the loud drumming of her heart and the thunderous stamping of her mount, as the once placid beast tore over the uneven ground, sending stones flying from beneath her hooves. The wind whipped Abigail's face, her watering eyes blurring her vision. One moment she was staring with terrified eyes between the horse's ears and the next, she saw heather and rocks and then the sky above her as she was catapulted from her saddle as the horse skidded to a stop so suddenly, she hadn't time to prepare herself.

She landed with an almighty crack, breaking the thin layer of ice atop a stream, the impact knocking the existing air from her lungs as her body slumped like a ragdoll, and she began slowly sinking as the freezing water dragged her down.

Chapter Twenty-Two

Edward kicked hard and his horse reacted, tearing after the run-away with Miss Dumont clinging for dear life to its back. He shouted her name and then realized there was probably no way she could hear him as with his horse's hoof beats ringing loud in his ears, so to must hers.   He loosened his rein, giving the large beast its head as he moved swift and sure, slowly lessening the distance. He was catching up, getting closer, waiting for that moment when he was close enough to grab her reins and could haul her from her mount, close her safe within his arms. *Would she swoon then? Look at him with adoration? Hero worship? Would she hold him close and kiss him?* He urged his horse onward, lying almost flat against the horse's neck. And then, all thoughts fled as he watched the woman he was in love with, leave the saddle, foot slipping loose of the stirrup, thank God, before she was airborne.

The loud crack as she landed echoed across the moor, the sound whipped up and carried on the wind. The weak winter sun chose that moment to slide behind a cloud and everything darkened!

How broken was she? He reined in his mount, gasping to catch a breath and dropped to the ground, running past her horse who snorted at him and stamped her foot. Abigail was nowhere to be seen, yet he'd watched her hit the ground, no, not the ground, the thin layer of ice that covered the stream, he ran forward his boots stomping on the shattered ice crystals and sinking a little in the boggy ground. The water was no longer a gentle meandering stream; after the storm yesterday, and the heavy rains throughout the night, the normally tiny stream was swollen, trebled in size and Miss Dumont was almost submerged. He stumbled, arms wheeling to regain his balance as the mud sucked at his boots, then splashed forward, reaching and grasping her coat, hauling the unconscious woman from the freezing water. "Miss Dumont, Miss Dumont" he called over and over as he placed a hand on her sternum and leaned close to her face. His eyes closed and he said a silent prayer of thanks as he felt her chest fall beneath his hand and a faint rasp of warm breath touch his cheek. She was alive but was most certainly not out of danger. He pulled at her coat, dragging the wet material down her arms, "Damn," he said, when he realized the rain resistant tweed was no match for the flowing stream in which it had been submerged. He tore his coat from his body and wrapped the drenched woman into it, praying the warmth from his body would linger, trapped in its folds, hoping it would be enough to keep her alive until he could get her home and warm again.

It was no mean feat to gather her into his arms and lift her with her sodden clothing, draping her over the front of his saddle before climbing up behind; he manhandled her until she was sat in front of him, her legs resting across his right thigh, her shoulders held firmly by his left arm as her head lolled then rested on his chest where he could feel the warmth of her breath.

The ride home seemed interminable, and he breathed a deep sigh of relief as the grey building appeared, tiny at first but grew quickly the closer they got. "Jackson," he bellowed as his mount walked along the carriageway. His man appeared in moments, taking in the two people atop his master's horse and the mare following despondently behind him.

"The mare startled," he said as Jackson held his horse still whilst he manoeuvred Miss Dumont and slipped, with a groan, from the saddle. He was chilled to the bone, his coat snug around the still unconscious woman, and his shoulders ached, both with the cold and from holding his precious cargo. He lifted her from the horse and carried her quickly across the forecourt and through the front door, up the staircase directly to her room.

"Bed warmers, Jackson. We need to warm her sheets. Then please see to the horses and then bring up some hot tea."

Jackson rushed around, filling the pan with glowing coals and thrusting it beneath the blankets, piled more logs into the grate and then he stopped, standing absolutely still as he watched Edward peel his coat from the frozen woman, as she lay, pale, on the rug. He shook his head knowing nought could be done, other than to undress the lass, to get her out of her wet clothing, and since there was no maid in residence... he let the thought drift as he left the room, leaving only the little Miss and the Master, closing the door behind him.

Edward finally succeeded in tugging his coat free, pulling it from beneath the wet gown, then he moved down to her feet, unlaced and removed her boots. Abigail lay unmoving, her face colourless except the tinge of blue around her lips, her breathing although rhythmic, barely lifted her chest. He began the laborious job of unbuttoning the jacket of the riding habit, cursing at the stiff material, made even less pliable after its dunking in the freezing water.

Finally able to pull the top aside, he began peeling it from her slender arms, he tugged the skirts down over her hip, her thighs, knees and finally pulled it free of her feet and discarded them in a soggy pile beside the motionless woman. The blouse, with its tiny, intricate buttons was next and his fingers, stiff and cold from the journey home and her wet clothes, made him fumble and he cursed. "Come on, man, they're just buttons." He chided himself, but the sound of his voice seemed to penetrate Miss Dumont's unconscious mind, and she whimpered seemingly in response, and her head rolled slightly. He continued to talk, telling her about the horses in the stables whilst he finished unbuttoning the last of her fastenings and withdrew everything from her body. She lay naked, on the mat and for a mere second all he could do was look upon the stunning beauty laid out before him. Then he was rushing to collect her towel from the fireguard, probably placed there to dry after her morning ablutions and began to rub gentle drying stokes across the skin on her flat stomach, the creamy skin of her breasts and then began a vigorous rub-down of legs and arms to dry and get the blood flowing, being careful to avoid the bandage. Leaving the towel draped across her body, he carefully removed the wrapping around her wound and threw the gauze into the flames, then he stood, shucking off his own shirt, then bent and lifted, cradling her in his arms. Her skin soft and still too cold against his stomach and chest. He carried her to the bed, gently laying her down and removing the heating pan from between the sheets, pulled the warmed blankets up and over her body.

He quickly stripped off the rest of his wet clothes and boots, moving to the fire, and rubbing his hands together to get the blood pumping. Glancing around he noticed a throw, covering the chair adjacent to the window, snatched it up and drew it around his shoulders and then made his way back to the bed where he perched near her pillows, sliding his cold feet beneath the blankets to steal some of the comfort warmth for himself and simply stared at the sleeping beauty before him as he continued his dialogue regarding his stables.

This was where Jackson found him a short time later. "Horses are all cared for, Sir. And I've bought ye the tea ye'd requested," he said tyring his hardest not to notice how very close his master was to the little Miss. "Err, I'm happy to sit for a while if ye want to run and dress," he said.

"In a moment, Jackson. I've been sitting here talking to Miss Dumont, it seems the sound of my voice stirs her a little, I'm positive her eyes fluttered just moments ago."

Jackson sauntered towards the bed and stared at the pale face of Miss Dumont. "Will she be okay, Sir?" She had been deathly pale when he'd last seen her, her poor lips had been blue, and her eyes darkly shadowed. He was happy to note there was a slight pinkening of her skin, the bluish tint had vanished and as he watched, she cracked open an eye and screamed.

<u>**Chapter Twenty-Three**</u>

Abigail was cold! She'd recalled snippets of the long ride back to the house seated in front of Mr Langley, his horse easily taking the weight of them both. The air had been frigid and burned her lungs on every inhale. The wind seemed to whip around the large form of Mr Langley, and no matter how much he'd attempted to covet her, the howling gusts found and froze the water in her gown and her boots. The smidgeon of heat from Mr Langley's coat had long since vanished. Her chattering teeth made her jaw ache, and the discomfort in her back and head throbbed from when she had fallen. It was all too much, and though she tried to stay awake, the numbness crept through the pain, and she found herself drifting back into unconsciousness.

Bright sparks of light hit Abigail behind her heavy lids, and she tried frantically to separate her lashes. Was there a fire? Oh Lord, please let it be a fire, she thought. The very inkling that there could be flames burning hot in the grate made her body tingle, or was that something else, something strange rubbing at her skin. Something abrasive, but, no, it must be the movement of the rough material of the riding habit. She whimpered, and the sound disappeared, swallowed by the darkness as it reached up and claimed once more.

Hot, she was burning. Oh God, the pain was intense. Every nerve ending sparking, coming back to life. She had to escape! Her eyes squinted open, and she screamed out her pain.

Stretched out beneath the covers, her poor body felt like it was being eaten alive, thousands and thousands of needle-sharp teeth, nipping, biting, she had to make it stop.

Three things happened simultaneously, Abigail suddenly lurched to a sitting position, the heavy blankets falling away and at the same time, the man who'd been sitting, leaning against the pillow on which she lay, toppled sideways, arms flailing as they flew from beneath the throw in which he was wrapped. He clutched at the closest thing to save himself and found his arms entwined with Miss Dumont's very naked torso. His bared chest pressed to her back, his smattering of chest hair, curling to tickle her smooth skin. And Abigail forgot all about the discomfort of her prickly, burning skin.

Abigail's eyes dropped to the bedcovers which now covered only her bottom half, tried to fathom why her arms had suddenly grown dark, curling hairs as they hugged her just below her breasts. She was so confused. What was happening? Her legs itched and felt like her skin was about to burst open, she moved, meaning to reach down to uncover her legs and realized the arms holding her, had not moved. She looked up, Jackson stood, the grimace on his good-natured face looked wrong, and she suddenly realized he was seeing her bared chest and her face flamed red. The heat at her back moved and she squealed as Mr Langley righted himself, slowly removing his arms and they stared, hypnotized by one another, neither of them moving, neither of them speaking. The silence settled heavy in the expectant air, just waiting, waiting to be shattered.

"Tea, Miss Dumont?" Jackson asked timidly.

Two sets of eyes spun in his direction, taking in the cup and saucer he held out. And then harried movement as Mr Langley leapt from the bed, losing his throw as he grappled with her blankets and hauled it back up to cover her naked breasts from the all-seeing eyes of his stable manager. And all Abigail could do was watch and catch her breath as she realized that Mr Langley was naked, leaning across her to hide her body and she couldn't pull her eyes away from the heavy club and tight balls that hung between two thick thighs.

"Thank you, Jackson, just leave it on the table," the naked man answered for her, as he hastily retreated and drew the throw around his torso, effectively hiding his erect manhood from view. Jackson nodded, trying to hide a smile as he set down the tea and quietly left the room, closing the door behind him.

"What are you doing?" Abigail spluttered at the man, eyeing the woollen throw. "Why are you in my bed? Why are you naked? Why am I? Who undressed me?" the questions poured from between her lips as her breath came out fast and faster the more wound up, she became.

"Please calm yourself. And believe me when I tell you, nothing inappropriate happened, I undressed you, Miss Dumont. There was no-one else except Jackson and, well, I thought maybe you'd rather I than he removed your wet clothing. If I had not, you would have frozen to death! My apologies, for your discomfort, but I'd rather you alive and angry than frozen and dead."

"But why are you...?" she flapped a hand toward him.

"I rescued you from the water, Miss Dumont. My trousers were soaked as were my boots. My shirt was wet from carrying you,," he explained, trying his hardest to calm the situation.

"You were in my bed, Sir!" she spat.

"Merely sitting beside your head, watching for signs of distress. Admittedly, my feet were beneath the covers soaking up some of the warmth, but, well, you must understand we could have both gotten gravely ill. I make no apology. Your health was always utmost in my mind."

He moved and brought the tea from the table and pushed the cup toward the fingers that still clutched at the bedclothes. She accepted it, clasping it tightly with her stiff fingers and took a sip. The sweet elixir settled her nerves, and not knowing what to say, she simply said. "Thank you, Mr Langley." He bowed, gripped the throw around his body a little tighter and made to leave the room.

"I'll have Jackson bring you food a little later, for now, I think sleep would be your best remedy," he said and closed the door.

Abigail settled back against the pillows where Mr Langley had sat. Oh my, what on earth was she to do now? That man had not only undressed her, looked upon her body and carried her to the bed, he'd stripped off his own clothing and joined her. Almost every wish in her heart had come true, and all of it whilst she'd been unconscious, her dream from the previous night had come back to haunt her. He'd been in her bed, and she'd seen, in broad daylight, Mr Langley's male anatomy; It certainly wasn't what she had expected. She'd heard rumours of red, ugly, bulbous members, and small barely there ones that her friends had tittered about behind their hands, but Mr Langley's had not been ugly; the pink, hard flesh had been hooded and stood to attention from a dark nest of curls.

She should feel embarrassed, he'd seen her naked and she'd seen him right back, but the only thing she felt was sadness that the encounter hadn't been created from love and desire, where they couldn't keep their hands off one another, their clothing ripped from each other in a passionate frenzy. Oh, she could dream; and dream she would with certainty, especially now she had a very vivid picture of the entirety of Mr Langley etched in her mind.

Alone now, she quickly drained the cup, tasting the brandy within, warm and rich on her tongue, and then heaved the blankets from her body. Her skin still felt tight, as though her blood had indeed frozen and then thawed within her veins, stretching them to near bursting; she must move, she needed to flex her aching arms and legs. Dropping the empty cup to the sheets she pressed herself upward, holding the bedframe for support just in case she was overcome and felt faint, for she could not call Mr Langley back to assist, were she to collapse! Or could she? A devilish voice said in her mind. Maybe... at least she would be awake to feel him lift her in those strong arms and play the hero for a second time; No. No, she could not! She stood, wriggled her toes, flexed her ankles, bending and straightening her knees before finally letting go of the bed, and took a slow walk around the room until the aches and tingles began to fade. Overall, she felt fine, except the constant throbbing around the egg-shaped bump at the back of her head. All in all, she'd survived her ordeal with very little injury. Her pride however, now that was a very different story.

Chapter Twenty-Four

Oh God, what had he done. Edward was pacing again.

On taking his leave of Miss Dumont, he'd dressed and paced, his mind whirling with thoughts of what he'd seen, what he'd felt, her skin so soft, but so cold beneath his fingers. How frantic he'd felt seeing her unconscious, he could not bear it.

And then, as she lay abed, her skin warming, the bluish-white flesh turning pink; the relief he'd felt, which very quickly turned to a yearning to climb in beside her, which he had. But his mind had continued with a fantasy of its own. The need to stroke the satiny smoothness of her breasts, to suck the pink tips between his lips until they were hardened nubs, to tease and taste the silken curls which hid that secret bud, which would see her writhe if he set his attentions to it. His cock was hard, straining, but he could not stop the pictures in his mind. He wanted Miss Dumont, badly.

And she had seen the evidence of his wantonness.

It pained him now to stay away from her. His body begging for release at the mere thought of her and for this very reason he knew he could not turn the knob on her bedroom door, though he paced the hallway outside of it many times during the course of the afternoon and evening. He'd tried to work in his study, but the figures on the pages he was looking at blurred until all he could see was the image of Miss Dumont as he'd released her from their shared kiss in this very room.

Jackson set a tray of food for him in the dining room, but he found his appetite was non-existent as he gazed at the chair in which she'd sat the night before, his fingertips itched to be touching her, to taste her mouth and now he knew the splendour of her body, he wanted his own mouth and body all over that silky skin.

By suppertime he'd almost worn a hole in the carpet. He'd done as promised and sent Jackson up to her with dinner but was disheartened by the responses to the questions he'd fired at the man. "How was she? Did she ask for him? Had she left her bed? But there was nothing to help him relieve his thoughts. Miss Dumont had answered the knock and requested the tray be left by her door. What was she thinking shut behind that wooden barrier? Was she thinking of him? Of his nakedness? Of his hands on her bare skin? Oh God, this was driving him crazy. His eyes shifted to the shelf which held the dark, golden liquid, beckoning him, taunting him with the promise to numb his discomfort. Pulling the stopper, he lifted the bottle to his lips and took a hefty slug, followed by another and another relishing the trail which burned, his tongue, his throat, his guilt. With each pull his brain quieted until a numbness crept over his limbs and his mind soon followed. He stumbled, cursing loudly as he fell up the stairs, his knees would be bruised come morning, but right now he felt no pain. He crawled, a much safer mode of transport, all the way to her bedroom and pushing the tray aside, food untouched as his had been, he sat, head resting on the cool, hard panelling, as close to her as he would allow himself, and closed his eyes.

He awoke with a startling jolt as the door behind him disappeared and for a moment it felt like he was airborne and then he was falling, falling backward his head slamming to the unforgiving hardwood floor with a resounding crack. That was certainly not going to help in any way the expected hangover. He lay with his eyes closed, groaning softly. Light shone red through his eyelids, and he wondered if he'd slept the night away and the sun already risen. He slowly, carefully cracked open his eyes and discovered Miss Dumont leant over him, a candle in hand which not only illuminated the space between them but outlined the curve of her breasts as they pressed against the thin fabric of her night shift.

"Mr Langley, what are you doing sitting at my door?" she admonished.

"I, I," he had no answer, the light from the candle felt like it was scorching his retina's and he huffed a breath, extinguishing the flame and leaving the room lit only with the orange glow from the burning logs in the fireplace. Without thought, he struck, snake like fast. Pulling her down, he held her close wrapping one arm around her waist and the other moved to cradle her head as his lips found hers, sipping, tasting, tongue plunging when her lips parted, and he was granted entry to her mouth.

He groaned, a deep rumble in his throat as he felt her relax into his embrace and her lips began to trace his with an unmistakable urgency. He rolled her beneath him, and felt her shiver, whether from the intimacy they shared or the hard wooden floor, he did not know; pushing up on his elbow he wrenching his lips from hers as his chest heaved, inhaling deeply, drawing the much needed air into his lungs, and with it, the most intoxicating scent; the sweetest of fragrances had him instantly hard. His craving for her intensified as he realized that the thin nightgown was all that separated him from the supple skin that had taunted him throughout the day, and from the source of her delicious scent. His lips skimmed the long slender column of her neck, sucking, licking, tasting his way down, his teeth grazing along her the swell of her breast and finding and tugging the ribbon on her shift, "so beautiful," he murmured as the material fell open baring her from shoulder to torso, one hand finding and caressing one silken breast whilst his lips nibbled down, down to find her nipple, he swirled his tongue over and around hardening the nub. Her sharp intake of breath filled her lungs, expanding her chest and pushing her breast harder against his lips as he opened his mouth wider, taking in more as his tongue flicked around her sensitive flesh. Abigail moaned, her fingers entwined in his hair, holding him in place as he sucked, and when he released her with a quiet pop, the sound in her throat was almost a sob. He moved his attention to her other breast and the sob changed back to a loud, aroused groan.

"Yes, oh, yes, Mr Langley," she whispered urging him on. Her hands fisting in his hair, as if she would never let him go. Her body writhed as his fingers walked down along the taut expanse of her waist, danced over the curve of her hips, down, down to her knees, before travelling in reverse, pinching at the thin cotton shift and trailing the material high, higher up to her thighs where he released it. He grinned around her nipple as a frustrated sigh left her lips and her body arched in search of him. He replaced his palm across the now exposed, pale skin and gliding his hand bypassed her sex, and he smiled again to himself at the whimper from her lips, telling him with no words, how she yearned for him to touch her. The shift rose higher as his hand continued to push up and up, staying only when the material bunched above her hips and in the soft glow of firelight, her thatch of curls glinting red at the apex of her thighs, calling to him, a call he could not refuse, he touched her. His hand stroked with purpose through the soft, damp curls, she was wet, he realized, wanting. He nudged her thighs apart and palmed her sex and he heard her draw in a shuddering breath and released it in a warm sigh which caressed his face, her fingers clenched in his hair, deliciously hurting, as she panted, her breasts rising and falling quickly, stimulated by his touch.

His mouth found hers again, wanting to capture every sound, her moans, the groans, the whimpers and the whispered 'Oh, oh, yes!" at the glide of his hand, as it skated, aided by her arousal over her bud and along the pouting, swollen lips of her sex. He captured her loud moan on his tongue as he slipped a finger between the silken folds and her hips bucked, spreading her legs further as he rubbed in and out of her heat, her breath quickened as she writhed, chasing, climbing, reaching for that elusive peak, always just out of reach, until suddenly it wasn't! Her body stiffened, her sex pulsed and clenched around his digit, and she cried out; and Edward gratefully swallowed every sound.

Chapter Twenty-Five

Abigail had never felt anything like it! Never in her wildest dreams, could she have imagined the feeling that coursed through her body.   How his hand cupped and rubbed through the slickness between her thighs, and then, oh god, his finger as it pushed inside of her. How the beating pulse of her heart, seemed to beat throughout her entire body, drumming along her nerves, tantalizing the very fibre of her most sacred parts, as they clenched around that dancing digit. Her hips raised, her legs seized, and she was thrust into oblivion, her muscles clenching so tightly, she held him in place as her body, erupted, white-hot explosive pleasure, she launched with a cry and then she was flying, flying.

Time stood still; she had no idea how high she flew but as her muscles relaxed, she felt herself floating gently, and then she was back, and through it all she could feel Mr Langley, his hand still cupping, his digit still inside her, and his lips swallowing her moans. She was very aware that she was nearly naked in his arms and that the insistent pressure bruising her hip, was Mr Langley's long, solid member; the knowledge that she was the cause of his erection satisfied her immensely. She floated in a sea of bliss. Sated. She was exactly where she was meant to be, held tight, warm and safe within his embrace.

Tiny, tender nips and nibbles at her lips, along her cheeks and down the slender column of her neck finally roused her. Bringing with it the awareness of the hard, uncomfortable floor beneath her shoulders, she wriggled them a little to ease the discomfort and then wished with all her being that she hadn't as Mr Langley stilled. Not a breath of movement for the longest time, and then to her dismay, he gently removed his finger, and pulled his hand away, untangling himself from her body. A whispered curse left his lips, as he scooped her off the floor and stood, walked with her cradled in his arms to her bed, where to her chagrin he laid her down and re-arranged her nightgown. Covering all the parts of her which were already aching for his touch again. As if he could read her thoughts, his dark eyes swept over her, as if memorising her feminine form by the light of the fire, filing away those moments they'd shared.

"Touch me, please" she pleaded, taking his hand where it hovered over the blankets, not able to bear the thought that he might leave before he made a real woman of her, before she could touch and explore his body too.

But he shook his head with a resigned sigh pulled his hand away, lifted the covers over her and turned away.

"Don't go," she whispered.

"I can't!" he exclaimed, "Miss Dumont. I …" his words deserted him, and he bowed his head and walked slowly, stiffly from the room as though to leave caused him great pain.

Abigail lay watching as he walked away, her heart so heavy within her chest it was almost suffocating her. What had she done wrong? Why had he turned away? He'd given her such a gift; the pleasure she'd felt would be remembered always. His touch lit a flame inside of her. She wanted it again, wanted it always with him. Only him. But even beneath the warm blankets, her body grew chilled, the gooseflesh rising on her arms as she realized with shocking clarity what she had just allowed to happen. Her thoughts turned to her family; what would they think of her? How could she ever return to them after she had freely let a man, a man who had laughed at the idea of being her husband, touch her so intimately? Tears threatened, her throat tightened, and she drew her arm across her eyes to hide the ambiance of the orange, flame lit room, and she wept. Wept for the loss of his hands upon her body, wept for a missed opportunity to lose herself entirely to the man she had fallen in love with, wept for the innocence which was barely touched and yet felt like it was now, forever lost to her.

How could she ever stay here? To be so close and yet so far apart from him. Knowing she'd spread herself for him, and instead of succumbing to the seductress beneath his hands, he'd made his feelings obvious; he walked away. He didn't want her.

Chapter Twenty-Six

God, he wanted her. He'd shuffled his way from her room, his arousal so damn hard it was difficult to walk.

He couldn't believe what he'd done, he'd been so close, so very close to taking her, and on the hard wooden floor of all places. She deserved so much better, a soft mattress, and pillows where her thick mane of auburn hair would cover the slip with its silken tresses.

He had wanted to sink into her, feel her cocoon his member as she had his digit, but even as she groaned her ecstasy, the thought of taking her completely before she knew how he felt, and the real reason he had brought her here, had him coming to his senses. The very senses that had been tossed aside the moment she'd opened her door and leant over him, the senses that took flight when his breath had doused the candle and at the same time lit a fire within his loins. He'd let her writhe on his hand while he hungrily kissed and captured the erotic sounds vibrating in her throat. He could almost taste her desire and heaven help him; he could still smell her sweet, sweet arousal from where she'd climaxed on his hand. His body shook with the need to bury more of himself inside of her; but lies and guilt, were his shackles, the chains that bound him, because she was here under false pretences. She was here because of a lie of his making. Because he wanted her to pay for the humiliation, she'd allegedly caused his cousin. God, his cousin! The guilt piled higher.

He should have sent her home!

No, he should never have brought her here to begin with. It was a stupid plan, it was cruel. He should have discovered the truth whilst still in London, where she was safely chaperoned by her parents. Would she have received him? She'd refused Spencer her time.

Miss Dumont wasn't cruel, she was a beautiful, passionate woman and he didn't believe for a moment, now that he'd gotten to know her, that she was capable of such treachery. She spoke the truth, so succinctly, he could attest to that; besides, what reason was there for her to shame and humiliate Spencer?

But someone had! They had spread untruths regarding him and Lord Dandion. Edward was no puritan, he knew things happened behind closed doors, but to have been called out as Spencer had been, damning him, damaging his good reputation, it could potentially mean social suicide. But if not Miss Dumont, then who could have discovered the incident, and been cruel enough to besmirch Spencer's good name?

Edward stripped down in the cold bed chamber, sluiced himself in the near freezing water, which Jackson had left much earlier in the evening; and finally, with the aid of the cold water and the heavy feeling of guilt and exhaustion, his arousal waned, and he pulled on a nightshirt, and slipped between the cold sheets. Tomorrow he would arrange for Miss Dumont to return to London. Once she was safely back with her family, he would find the truth for Spencer, and he would pursue Miss Dumont for himself. Guilt or not, he was no longer ready to sacrifice his own happiness for the sake of his cousin. It would be every man for himself.

Edward felt he'd hardly closed his eyes when a sharp knock sounded at his door. He cracked his eyes open very slowly, the light coming through the gap in the curtains, blinding, to his sleep-deprived, alcohol induced, red-rimmed eyes.

"Morning, Sir." Jackson called as he dragged the heavy material back to reveal the orange and red fire in the sky as the sun rose. "Ye've slept through breakfast and Mr Fletcher is waiting in the study for ye."

"God," Edward groaned. "What's the bloody time?" he rubbed his hand absently over his bristly face and knuckled the sleep from his eyes.

"It's gone eight. I see the whiskey was out to play again last evening, should I be worried, lad?"

"No," Edward said on a sigh, and when Jackson gave him side-eye he repeated with a "No, not at all. I , hssss," he hissed as his toes touched the cold wood, and he stood up. "Jackson, I'll be needing you to escort Miss Dumont back to town. I appreciate it's a short notice, but I insist that she must return home immediately."

Jackson looked startled. "Today, Sir? But I thought…" his words came to a halt, and he simply stared at his young master. Seeing the sickly grey pallor of his skin from his over-indulgence, the red-lined eyes from lack of sleep and the determined set to his features, and the words died on his lips, instead he replied, "Yes, Sir, I'll prepare the carriage right away and request Miss Dumont pack her things." He shook his head as he walked away, realizing that something had happened to push the younger man to this decision. He only hoped that Miss Dumont had not been hurt.

Once Jackson had gone, Edward quickly shivered through another freezing sluicing and surprisingly felt almost human as he dressed and then trotted down the staircase and entered the study.

"Francis," Edward greeted his friend with a slap on the back. "you're out and about early."

"Well, I can't say the same of you, old chap, what's the to-do lying abed till all hours? Or have you got a woman in there with you, keeping you warm and awake all night, eh?" he grinned and gave Edward a lecherous wink. "Maybe a pretty red head perhaps?"

"Indeed, it was a reddish colour alright, but it came in a bottle, and I drank an awful lot of it." Edward responded. "And I've got a hell of a head on me to show for it. So, let's be getting to business; shall we head to the stables?"

The two men strolled toward the back door, where Edward shrugged into his old woollen overcoat, frowning a little when he felt the warmth within its folds, someone had recently worn his coat, a warm glow spread through him, it had to have been Miss Dumont, and he glanced surreptitiously round the kitchen in hopes of a glimpse of the love of his life. Sadly, she was nowhere to be seen. He reached for the door, noting it was still unhinged and wondered if Jackson had come back from the stables already, while Frances droned on about the evils of the bottle. As he turned to pull the door closed behind them a blur of auburn moved past the kitchen doorway, vanishing as swiftly as it appeared, and suddenly there was silence.

"You still have 'the maid' staying then." Francis said, his eyebrows rising and falling almost comically. "Mayhap it wasn't just the whiskey bottle after all, you sly dog, you."

Edward said nothing but led the way from the house towards the stable, his face flushed, knowing he'd been caught but unwilling to concede that there had indeed been a smidgeon more than whiskey he'd gotten drunk on. But then he wasn't about to elaborate to his friend what had occurred between him and the delectable auburn-haired beauty.

Francis chuckled at the red flush on Edward's face. "I wonder if it's genetic, this love of fiery redheads!" Edward stared at him, what did he know? "Don't you think it strange that both you and your cousin have a preference to red haired beauties. I attended a soirée at Lady Devonish's, and noticed Spencer had a stunning young redhead on his arm. I had heard that he's proposed marriage to her," a strangled laugh left his lips. "He'll have his hands full, what with a wife and a lover."

"Spencer doesn't keep a mistress." Edward said, but he was beginning to have a bad feeling about this conversation.

"Who said anything about a Mistress. Mayhap you don't know your cousin as well as you thought..."

"Oh, come now Francis, surely you've not been listening to this insane gossip?" Edward interrupted.

"It's not gossip if it's true. I mean, he did have Lord Dandion tailing him from the library. The woman all dishevelled pulling down her gown, your cousin trying to return his cock to his trousers and Julian looking stary-eyed. I didn't know Spencer had it in him," he laughed again although there was little humour in it, "I'm guessing he probably did have it in him," he repeated his face serious and then without missing a beat or noticing how Edward's hands had fisted, or the furious glint in his eye, asked, "Have you met her?"

Edward ignored his question, instead asking one of his own. "Are you telling me that you saw the three of them, together?"

"Indeed, I watched the three of them fleeing the library. My thought was that someone had come upon them in their um, compromising positions, and made a dash for it," he replied with a grim smile.

"And where were you? Was anyone else around when they made their escape from the library?" Edward asked tightly.

"I'd been entertaining," he replied, his eyebrows raised and a cold, bitter expression on his face. "I was in the study opposite and heard a bit of a commotion, so stepped to the door to see what was going on. I had front seat tickets to the show. Though I don't believe anyone else noticed."

"So, YOU are the only person to have witnessed them. Who did you tell, Francis?" he asked through gritted teeth.

"Tell? Why, I um, I may have mentioned it to old Lucas, down at the club, he had quite a laugh about it. Oh and of course the couple of young maids I had," he paused, tongue-in-cheek, "been servicing," he chortled. "Get it, Service? Maid?" His good humour was quickly doused when Edward's fist flew hard and fast striking Francis with a satisfying crack.

"God, it was you. You're the one spreading the rumours!" Edward raged.

"What the hell," Francis shuffled back a few steps to regain his balance as his hand flew to his face, catching the blood which began to pour with earnest from his nose.

Edward followed him and struck again, then again until Francis lost his footing, Edward followed him down to the frozen ground, his fist still meting out punishment for all the hurt and destruction that had occurred because Francis had been unable to keep his bloody mouth shut.

Chapter Twenty-Seven

Abigail hadn't slept a wink. She had never felt so bereft as she had when Mr Langley had walked away. She lay where he'd left her, the blankets up to her chin, but the chill remained. The fire in the grate died down to a glowing ember, the comparison not lost on Abigail, her own fire had burned hot and bright for such a small amount of time, and she had basked in the glow from the ember he'd ignited within her and then he left, and just like the fireplace, all the heat had seeped away and left only cold, lifeless ashes.

She knew she could never face him, not now, maybe never and so she made her decision. She rose, and quickly washed, not even noticing the bite of the cold water on her skin; Dressed and then began to quickly fold her meagre belongings, pressing them neatly into her trunk. The gown Mr Langley's large fingers had torn a panel from and still bore scorch marks, she'd left discarded in the corner of her old room. She would not be retrieving it; besides it was unable to be repaired, and the memories it invoked were not something she wished to take with her on her journey back to her home, back to her parents, back to the loneliness their house had become as her siblings grew and left the family home Her brothers had long since boarded a sailing ship for far off lands, searching for adventure, and her sister too would soon be leaving, her wedding date to Mr Ashcroft drawing inexplicably closer.

But, with no place left to go, return she would, broken-hearted and not quite as innocent as when she'd left. How was she to hold her head up and explain to her father that she'd run away; after all, she was the currency that was to repay his debt. But not only that, her father had been positive that a union would be formed between herself and Mr Langley. Her mother must have expected there to be a betrothal, surely that was the only reason her mother had allowed her to go unchaperoned to Mr Langley's home. Yet, she would return, unwed, alone, and for the rest of her days dream of what might have been if only Mr Langley had fallen in love with her as she had him.

Hiding in her room and wishing were hardly conducive to escaping, although the thought of leaving him pained her, the thought of seeing him again burned her. After all but begging the man last night, he'd made his feelings blatantly clear when he walked away.

No, she shook her head, she had to stop this, it would get her nowhere. She would plead her case to Jackson. Surely, he would be her ally and aid in her getaway. She took a deep breath and opened her door, checked all was clear and crept noiselessly along the hallway and down the stairs.

She'd barely stepped off the staircase when she heard men's voices by the front door. Her heart began to pound and with one hand pressed to her chest, with the other she lifted her skirt and ran to the nearest room, a cold deserted room with a single cot bed. How strange that of all the places to hide, it would be in the small bedchamber in which she'd huddled, frozen and afraid during her first night in Cornwall. She hid herself behind the door, straining her ears to catch the conversation. Jackson was talking about horses, and when the other man answered, it wasn't the rich baritone of Mr Langley, but the bassy growl of Mr Fletcher; whom she most definitely didn't want to see again, the weaselly, uncouth man; she thought pressing her body further against the wall, wishing to make herself invisible.

"Edward should be expecting me," he was saying, although it sounded more like a scolding as if it was Jackson's fault that the master of the house was still abed.

"Aye, well, if ye'd take a seat in the study, I'll go right now and rouse 'im." Jackson steered the surly man towards the study and once Francis had taken his seat, she heard Jackson move back toward the staircase. She gasped aloud when his head popped around the door and he gave her a wink, and whispered, "Good Mornin', Miss, I suggest ye leave breakfast until after the gentlemen have vacated the premises." And then his head disappeared, and she heard him climb the stairs.

She silently rounded the door, tiptoeing past the closed study door toward the kitchen. If she could have held her bladder, she would have done as Jackson bid and stayed hidden in her old room, but the freezing temperatures had her crossing her legs, she needed to use the outhouse and she needed to go now. Releasing the breath she'd held, she reached the back door, wincing a little as she turned the old brass key in the lock, and the heavy-set door squeaked as she pulled it open. The sky was clear, and she was sure it would turn into another sunny day, but right now a frigid wind slapped her cheeks with a painful, burning cold, and she shivered; it was freezing out there! She swung the door too and snagged the large, wool spun coat from the hook, snuggling it around her shoulders, warming her instantly, and she pulled the door ajar again just enough for her to squeeze through, slipped out and pulled it quietly back into place.

Holding the coat lapels tightly in one hand, and lifting her gown with the other, she ran.

The outhouse was no warmer, but at least the wind couldn't reach her, it merely whistled its eerie tune, making the naked twigs on the tree branches dance and scratch against the outer walls of the privy. She shivered as she sat, her thoughts on home and the inside plumbing her father had paid handsomely for, when the sound of footsteps passing close by had her holding her breath, ears straining, but there was nothing to hear, no conversation, just the fading of the footfalls and then silence. She hurried herself, patting down her gown and pulling the coat more securely around her shaking shoulders, then surreptitiously checking the coast was clear, she darted up the path.

Getting back inside the house was more of a mission. She needed to first check that the back door and kitchen were clear of the three men. She hadn't been out for long, would Jackson still be upstairs with Mr Langley, or had that been him walking past, ready to start his day in the stables? And what of Mr Fletcher, was he still waiting in the study? She had to be certain and so she made her way along the wall, her shoes slipping a little on the icy path, she peered inside the warm, cosy kitchen. No one, no movement at all except the fire flickering in the hearth, bidding her to enter and warm herself. She hurried back, opened the door with its complaining squeak and squeezed inside, slipping the coat from her shoulders she reached for the hook and froze! Voices! Loud, clear and heading her way. There was no time, the coat snagged the hook as she moved quickly, the door left unlatched and slightly ajar. She rushed toward the pantry, hunkered down behind the flour sacks and potato buckets, her breath pounding in her ears as she pressed her hand to her lips to help subdue the miniscule sound her seemingly loud exhales made. Just in time too as she spied Mr Langley and his friend, as they made their way across the kitchen discussing, of all things, the downfalls of imbibing too much alcohol. It hurt to see him, cut her that she meant so little to him that he was here discussing something so mundane when she could think of nothing but him, his hands and lips on her body last night. She couldn't help it, a sob rose in her throat, and she knew the sound would burst from her lips, she swallowed again and again holding it back, her eyes brimming until finally Mr Langley moved out of the kitchen and Abigail made a dash from her hiding place to the hallway in a blur of movement, quickly running back into the frigid temperatures of her former bed chamber where she sat on the cot, covered her face with her hands and let the tears fall.

This was how Jackson found her! "Aw come now, Miss. Don't ye be crying," he said gently pulling a clean cloth from his pocket. "'ere now, dry ye're eyes. Are ye injured?" he asked his eyes flicking over her form as she huddled on the cot.

She shook her head, no. Then changed her mind and nodded. "Yes, in here," she said and touched her chest. Jackson eyed her sympathetically, she looked so very young, so vulnerable, he felt for her and for his young master too.

"Aye, I know it," he agreed. "I didn't expect it mind, but I've watched both of ye o'er the last few days."

"I must go; I can't face him again. Will you help me?" she begged. "I've packed my things, I'm ready now. Please say yes!"

Jackson looked surprised. He'd been dreading having to tell her that she must pack so he could drive her home; knowing there would be tears, but this was quite an unexpected turn of events.

"Of course, Miss. I'll gladly assist any way I can. Ye're all packed ye say?" and at her nod he continued. "Right then, I'll collect your luggage if you'll squirrel away some food for the carriage ride. Ye've not yet broken yer fast. I'll meet ye at the front door." He went to turn but stopped and looked back at her, "Ye'll not be saying farewell to the master then?" He inquired, hoping to glean a little information to what had gone so wrong last night.

Abigail shook her head. "The good-byes have been said," she sniffled, aching at the memory of how he'd tucked her in and strode stiffly from her room, "how long before we can set off? I don't wish to be here when Mr Langley and Mr Fletcher return."

"We'll be away in a jiffy, Miss. The carriage is ready and waiting. I'll collect ye're bags this minute."

"Oh, I didn't mean to impose, if you've readied the carriage for …"

"Don't fret yourself, Miss," he interrupted. "Mr Langley called for me to ready the carriage, his orders were for me to take ye home."

"I, I see," she stuttered. The words slicing her heart, sharp and agonising. Not only had he shunned her advances last night, but this morning he'd decided to be shut of her completely. She blinked, fighting back tears and said, "very well, I shall hurry to the kitchen for supplies. I wouldn't wish to overstay my welcome."

Moving past him, she returned to the kitchen and proceeded to wrap bread, cheese, and biscuits, packing them carefully into a large basket she found in the pantry, along with two bottles of wine which she seized from the shelf, and a glass.

Within a half hour, she was seated inside the cosy carriage and as Jackson called to the horses, and the wheels began to spin, she found herself leaning forward to stare from the window at the vast, grey house, one she no longer feared, and yes, had secretly visioned herself as one day becoming its mistress. As they drew away, she knew deep in her heart, she would never see the place or its owner again. She sat back in her seat and pulled the curtain across the small window; she couldn't bear to watch as the building disappeared from view as the carriage rocked its way over the shifting stones.

<u>**Chapter Twenty-Eight**</u>

Edward stared across at Francis where he lay on the frigid ground, hand to his face, a deep groan coming from his throat.

"Mr Fletcher? Christ, Mr Fletcher what happened? Are you alright, Sir?" Seymour, the groom that Francis had sent ahead to the stables, was running across the frosty grass and skidded to a stop beside the two men.

"Help me up, Seymour," Francis said, his voice sounding like he was underwater. He leant to the side and spat, spraying the frozen ground with a fountain of red. Seymour held his hand to his employer and gingerly aided him in gaining his feet. Francis looked down at Edward, a handkerchief over his rapidly swelling nose. "Why?" was all he managed to choke out.

Edwards voice was cold when he responded. "You have no idea the hurt you've caused by spreading your malicious gossip. I don't know what Spencer did to deserve such hostility from you. Your rumours, they've had him shunned from clubs, literally turned away at the door. Folk have turned away when he walks by, it's like he is diseased, and people are too frightened to be near him for fear of contracting something.

Spencer is not and has never been in any kind of relationship with Lord Dandion! He is very much in love with Miss Dumont and if she will still have him, intends to continue with his proposed nuptials. And..." he took a deep breath, trying to rein in his anger, before continuing.

"And, if that isn't enough, you've made me do something outrageous in my search for the damned cur and here you are, my own friend and right under my very nose. I can't believe you'd be so callous Francis."

Francis rocked, a little on unsteady feet while he stared down to where Edward still sat, "Edward, I'm sorry, I wasn't thinking straight, it was a shock to see Julian and Spencer together like that." He spat again to clear away the blood trickling down to the back of his throat. "But what's to be done?"

"There is nothing to be done. To attempt to bring the truth out will simply keep the lie alive! Spencer is staying quiet, waiting for the gossips to get bored, and move on to the next poor bastard who gets caught with his pants down." He stood and wiped the moisture from his coat. "I have somewhere important to be. Here Seymour, take your master's other arm." And between the two, they led Francis across the grass and into the warmth of the stables where the horses whinnied a greeting to the men.

Edward was impatient, he had to stop Jackson before he took Miss Dumont back to London. The two men mounted their horses and once Edward had attached lead rope and handed one off to Seymour and sending him ahead. He turned to Francis and as he handed him the rope, he said, "I won't tell Spencer it was you, so long as you stay well away from any of my family," he slapped the stallion on which Francis sat, and not waiting a moment longer, turned toward the house; sprinting across the sparkling grass, ignoring the beauty of the sun catching the icy crystals and shoved open the door. "Miss Dumont!" he shouted. "Jackson?" Silence greeted him, as he bounded up the staircase and burst, without knocking, into Miss Dumont's room. "Damn!" he exclaimed when he found it cold and empty. She was gone, left without a goodbye.   He slumped heavily onto the unmade bed and dropped his head to his hands. How could he have been so stupid, why'd he let her go? With a groan he slipped sideways, drew his feet onto the mattress and grasping the pillow to his face, inhaled the sweet floral scent which was purely Miss Dumont, and he groaned. What a mess he'd made of things!

Now that he knew the truth; knew that it was Francis who'd spread the ugly words and not Miss Dumont, he could have … Could have, what? What could he have done? Not sent her away. Tear up the chit that he held in his study. Tell her the truth, that he'd tricked her and then seduced her, even when he knew she was his cousin's intended?

He sat up, still clutching the pillow, and made a snap decision, because, hell, he knew how those kinds of decisions turned out, but he didn't care. He had to find her! Had to tell her that her father was indeed the person she'd always thought. Edward would not ruin her perception of him as a doting father and a kind and good husband, for a moment more; he would take the chit her father had drunkenly signed, and he would tear it to shreds before her very eyes.

He would explain, or try at the very least, without embarrassing her further about the rumours, how they affected her fiancé. That is if she still wanted Spencer; because that look in her eyes last night and the breathy sighs, the moans of ecstasy as she found her release at his touch, were surely not the actions of a woman in love with another. Love? Had she ever truly been in love with Spencer? And yet last night, almost begged for his own touch? Could she possibly have feelings for him? And would the truth and his declaration of love be enough to woo her back to his arms? So many questions with so little answers.

He knew one thing for certain, he wasn't going to win her back by sitting and thinking about it. He stood and took one last, deep inhale of her lingering scent and then threw the pillow back to the bed and strode from the room. His first stop the study, where he retrieved the chit and pushed it into his pocket, and then he was running back to the stables to saddle his horse. Surely the carriage could not have gotten too far. With a foot in the stirrup, he swung his leg across the wide back of his mount and with a swift nudge with his heels, the horse's hooves thundered down the carriage way and onto the road.

Chapter Twenty-Nine

Abigail eyed the bottles that clinked together with the movement of the carriage, chink, chink. Chink, she leant forward meaning to adjust their positions in the basket but froze with her hand around the neck of the nearest; 'it's far too early to be drinking,' her mother's voice echoed in her mind. How many times had she heard that when her father had poured himself a glass before luncheon? "I wasn't going to drink it mother, I was moving it," she muttered to the woman in her head. The woman whom she was returning to, who would surely notice the difference in her youngest daughter. Notice and judge! She wouldn't sympathise with Abigail over her broken heart, no, she would be judged on how she'd ruined a perfect opportunity to gain a husband. She gripped the bottle and pulled it from its resting place and tugged the cork free; retrieved the glass and poured with difficulty as the carriage rocked, then the glass touched her lips, and she gulped back its entire contents. The wine was flavoursome, sweet, palatable; unlike the whiskey that Mr Langley had thrust upon her, that had made her cough and splutter and had her body reacting with a shudder. No, this was easy on the tongue, cooling as it coated her parched throat, and she recalled she'd neither eaten nor had her morning cup of tea today. The glass emptied quickly and was refilled. Her tears dried, and the drafty carriage began to warm. She pushed the woollen throw from her knees, and it pooled at her feet. The sadness which had threatened to drown her waned and the sharp edges of her broken heart were not cutting quite so painfully as she poured her third glass. Her mind blanketed by the sweet wine, it numbed the pain and the sadness, replacing it with an unexpected calmness. By the fourth glass she couldn't figure whether it was the carriage that was swaying or just her, the movement making the wine in her belly swish and slop and she giggled in delight at the funny sound it made. She made to refill for the fifth or was it the sixth or… she'd lost count, and she grinned, not able to supress the silly smile plastered on her face as she tipped the bottle, gave it a bit of a shake and then closing one eye peered into the opening to find it was indeed empty. She dropped the depleted vessel and leaned forward to retrieve the second bottle when the carriage skidded to a stop and Abigail, with a shriek slid to the floor. She didn't know why they'd stopped so suddenly and honestly, she didn't care. The carriage may have stopped but the swaying hadn't, so she stayed where she was and tugged out the cork, refilling her glass again and had just raised it to her lips when the door was flung open. Cold air rushed in, and Abigail giggled loudly up at Mr Langley from her position on the carriage floor. She laughed aloud as she took in his wind tousled hair and cold reddened nose and cheeks, but most of all from his muttered expletive.

"Damnation!" he exclaimed. "Jackson, what is the meaning of this?" he called out, not taking his eyes off her as she tipped the glass and drained it then began to pour another. Jackson peered around the door, and she smiled wide and waved the bottle at him. He couldn't repress the grin that flashed across his lips as he took in her pity party for one, spread on the floor of the carriage, just like she was having a picnic.

"Want shome, Jakshon." She slurred blinking her eyes as the friendly man swayed and blurred before her unfocused gaze. She giggled again, "shtand shtill, you're making my tum…" her eyes widened, and she dropped the bottle and put a hand to her mouth. Suddenly there was movement everywhere as Mr Langley leaned in and gripped her waist, dragged her forward to the door and literally swung her through the opening, whilst turning her swiftly away from him; her head spinning, her stomach recoiling and then she was on her knees on the road and the wine made its second appearance. Her eyes streamed, her nose ran, and her throat burned as her stomach muscles spasmed, expelling its contents onto the road. Her chest heaved and she moaned softy, and when a hand gently rubbed her back, she recoiled from it as if burned.

"Don't touch me," she spat. All her calm and good humour now lay in the puddle of regurgitated alcohol on the stones. The pain she'd felt was back full force, but instead of self-pity; anger raged instead. "That invitation has been revoked." She stood unaided and wiped her face with her coat sleeve and stood shivering in the cold, late morning air.

"Miss Dumont, my apologies, I meant only to assist, please let me help you back into the carriage, it's far too cold to stay outside." Edward held his hand out to her again, but she ignored it.

"I don't need anything from you, Mr Langley! I'm quite sure I can manage on my own," she moved away from him but was relieved to see Jackson standing beside the door. She noted the step he'd set for her and nodded her thanks as he helped her into the carriage. She also noted that the bottle, and glass had been removed and only a wet patch indicated where her wine had spilled. Jackson closed the door behind her, and she sat letting her head fall back against the rest, and closed her eyes; the carriage spun, and she opened them again quickly and dropped her face into her hands. Her stomach may have purged the wine, but she was still drunk.

Mr Langley was here! What possible reason could he have for following her? He'd wanted her gone; she'd complied. Had he changed his mind, decided she needed to fulfil her repayment of the debt? That most assuredly would be too cruel. To see him, to want him so badly would only magnify the pain in her chest. She sat waiting, drowning in her inner dialogue and prayed for the carriage to once again, take her far away from the source of her pain.

<u>**Chapter Thirty**</u>

Miss Dumont disappearing from his sight sent a jolt through his chest. The tightness which had held him in its stead all morning released as he'd peered through the open carriage door, just to lay eyes on her beautiful face was enough to soothe his aching heart, but now with the door once more closed against him, that fist squeezed tightly around his heart once more.

The shock of seeing her laughing at him, drunk as a lord. Her eyes glazed and lips spread wide in a gleeful smile had momentarily taken his breath, stopped him dead in his tracks. God, he loved her so much.

But then reality struck; She was drunk because of what he'd done. She was on her knees in the road, for God's sake, all because of him, but even then, he couldn't resist the temptation to touch her, to stroke her back to help ease the tension of her shoulders. It almost broke him as she pulled away, snapping at him about the rescinded invitation, as in his mind he saw her as she'd lain last night, eyes bright, lips plump and bruised from their kisses, her whispered words, 'touch me'. A plea which he'd ignored, walked away with no explanation. It was no wonder she'd want nothing to do with him now.

He turned towards Jackson and groaned, "What do I do? She's innocent."

Jackson stared at him confused. If he was correct in his assumption of what transpired between the two last night, she was no longer innocent. But then Edward continued, and he realized he was not talking about last night at all.

"I found him, Jackson, the bastard behind the rumours. It was Francis! The culprit was right under my nose the whole time and I, I could only see her, to blame her for hurting Spencer and now," he ran his hands through his hair, "now, I've exacerbated the situation. Not only have I hurt Miss Dumont, but quite possibly, if he discovers my actions, alienated my cousin. I didn't mean to fall in love with his fiancé, and I certainly had no intention to lay hands on her; but damn it all, I need her. I want to steal her away from the very man my intentions were to aid. What do I do? I've made such a mess!"

"The only thing ye can, lad. Explain; give her yer story and see how it sits." Jackson looked on pityingly, he couldn't see this ending well at all.

Edward blew out a deep breath, then gripped the handle and pulled the door wide open. She sat with her head in her hands but startled at his appearance, her face paling as he stepped up, causing the carriage to rock quite alarmingly. He sat opposite Miss Dumont, and she stared at him in horror.

"Miss Dumont, I feel I owe you an explanation," he stated, voice low and apologetic, his shoulders tensing as she turned angry green eyes on him.

"I disagree," she replied tersely. "I can think of nothing you can say that I would wish to hear." She turned away to stare out of the window.

Edward leant his head back against the carriage for a moment, trying to organise his thoughts, his words. Then pushing his hand inside his coat, he pulled out the signed piece of paper and laid it across her knees. "I made a mistake, Miss Dumont. This agreement was signed under false pretences, there was no debt. Your father wasn't gambling the night I met him. He was simply drunk, drowning his sorrows and complaining about the alleged misconduct of my cousin. For you to understand my actions, you must know that my family means everything to me. I was furious when I discovered how my cousin had been treated, and so I took advantage of your father's inebriation to infiltrate your family. It was wrong, I know that. I battled with myself all that night over what I'd done and had decided to be honest with your father and tear up the contract," he pointed to the paper and shook his head. "I wanted to forget it all; but then I saw you, Miss Dumont, peering through the stair rail, and my mind was changed again."

"I don't understand! Why would seeing me change your mind," her voice small and hopeful, had he felt something for her as she had him?

"Your appearance was my undoing I'm afraid; I wondered if you'd hidden yourself on the staircase when Spencer called and watched whilst he was turned away. It was callous of me, I know, but I thought to teach you a lesson in empathy, perhaps assist in rebuilding your character to be as beautiful as your face." He watched the hope disappear from her eyes, as her face flushed a deep red, her blood boiling at his words and he knew he was in more trouble.

"How dare you, Sir. You knew nothing of my character, you had never met me. What right did you have to judge me on a glimpse?" Her bosom heaved, and his eyes followed the movement, remembering how wonderful her breasts felt pushed into his palms, his mouth. He quickly looked back to her face, raising a hand to halt her next verbal attack and spoke quickly.

"My cousin had coloured you as Aphrodite; a goddess, or a witch with those bewildering green eyes. He was bewitched by you, under your spell, and I was determined you would be made to suffer as he was." Abigail must have been more drunk than she realized because she had no idea who he was talking about. She stared dumbfounded as he continued his rambling explanation. "I used the pseudo-chit to steal you away to enact revenge for Spencer. I wished to humiliate you, as my cousin and his family were humiliated by the ugly rumours which I believed you had spread. But I was wrong! I've since discovered Francis was the guilty party, you were innocent all along." Her eyes blazed and the look of confusion on her face halted whatever he was going to say next. He wasn't explaining this very well at all.

She sat listening, but not hearing, not understanding anything except the words, '*I wished to humiliate you*'. Humiliate! He had deliberately set out to humiliate her for some reason to do with his cousin. She thought back to the day she'd arrived, when he'd saved her from the fire; was it humiliation he'd expected from her as she awoke on his dining table, was that why he'd spread her like a feast for him to devour? Was his command to dine with him the following day, meant to demean, and deprive her of her free will? Should she have been embarrassed and ashamed when she regained consciousness after nearly freezing to death, with him naked in her bed? And was the way he made her feel, his mouth on her breast, his fingers finding her warm, wet centre all a ploy to humiliate her? A sob broke from her throat.

"You wanted to humiliate me?" her whispery voice low, filled with pain and despair. "You made me feel for you, whilst you laughed behind my back. Oh, how you must have congratulated yourself when I allowed your touch, shared kisses and intimacies with you. It's crystal clear now why you walked away, leaving me wanting, because it was the ultimate humiliation wasn't it, leaving me begging?" Her green eyes were stormy seas as she tossed her head back, some of the pins slipping free of her hair and she shoved the auburn tresses behind her ear as she leant forward and snatched the paper from where it lay on her gown and with a vicious tug, tore it in two.

"No, never…," he cried, "not last night. Last night was precious, you were all I dreamt you'd be, but it was never meant to happen, I got carried away, but you were so beautiful and I couldn't resist," he watched her jaw tighten and quickly bit off the rest of his thoughts, continuing instead with, "what we did last night, was most certainly not meant to humiliate. " He could see by the cold uncompromising look on her face that she didn't believe him. And why would she? Instead of honouring her plea to touch her, to love her, he'd turned and walked away. And, if her body had felt anything like his, needy and aching for more; she must have burned with the sting of his rejection.

He should have told her how much he admired her, how very much he'd come to love her and asked her to be his wife; but he had done none of these things. He'd left her, alone. He could concede to himself now, witnessing the pain she was in, that he had made the gravest mistake of his life. She would never forgive him.

"Get out, Mr Langley, get out, get out!" She screamed, the pitch rising, the volume, so very loud in the confines of the carriage it left his ears ringing. What could he do other than comply? He pushed the door wide and stood, ducking his head and stepped down to the road. He turned as she leant forward and grasped the window ledge, pulling the door towards her, "Please take me home, Jackson," her voice pleaded and then she closed the door, figuratively and literally shutting him out in the cold.

Jackson looked down at him from where he perched, reins in hand and slowly shook his head, a silent apology showing on his face as he flicked his wrist, and the horses stepped off.

"Don't leave! I'm sorry!" Edward yelled as the wheels barely missed his foot, moving the carriage and its precious cargo away from him. "I love you, Miss Dumont."

His words echoed, unanswered, in the late morning air. And he watched as the carriage continued to pull away, taking her further and further away from him. And even as the echo of the horses' hooves, the crunching pebbles beneath the wheels and the jangle of the harness had long since faded, he still stood unable to believe she was really gone. Only when his horse nudged his back, causing him to nearly stumble did he turn away and climb, wearily and stiffly into the saddle, clinging to the pommel as the horse trod the path back towards his cold, empty home.

Back at the stables, routine took control as Edward found himself rubbing down his sweat-soaked horse and adding oats to the feed bin. Manual labour kept his arms moving, his hands busy and his mind numb. Once the work was completed, the stalls shovelled, and fresh straw spread, feed bins and water troughs filled, he left the horses behind, knowing they would be fine for the day and trudged reluctantly to the house.

The walls had never looked less inviting, and the emptiness smacked him in the face as he walked through the door. The study beckoned, or rather, the bottles he knew were on the shelf did. It was just what he needed, just a sip to warm his insides and the rest to numb the crushing pain in his chest. His need to be close to Miss Dumont overrode his comfortable chair, and with bottles in hand, he clomped his booted feet up the staircase and into the room where not only had he helped her find her pleasure but had unintentionally humiliated her after the fact. He hung his head at his own stupidity, he didn't deserve her. Taking a healthy swig of the amber liquid; its fiery heat quickly licking at his throat, then he took another swig and another. Moving slowly, he sat on her bed, his back against the sweet-smelling pillows, eyes staring, booted feet messing the sheets and he drank. One bottle dropped to the floor and a second was opened before his eyes closed and an alcohol induced sleep, pulled him under.

He woke shivering, groaned and turned over. Her scent still lingered on the pillows, and he inhaled deeply, remembered she was gone. His fingers gripped the neck of the bottle. He brought it to his lips and drank in long, hard pulls before flinging the empty vessel at the fireplace, not caring as the glass shattered and rained to the floor. Not caring about anything. He scrambled beneath the blankets, closed his eyes and drifted back into oblivion.

Chapter Thirty-One

Abigail sat stiffly as the carriage did it's best to rock her from her seat. How could she bare this for four days, with only the sound of the wheels bouncing over stone and the fast-paced clip, clop of the horses' hooves for company? Simple answer; she couldn't. The quiet gave her far too much time to think, to brood and to grieve what she'd left behind.

She was hurt and confused. Her mind raced as she tried to piece together his words. Francis, she knew was Mr Fletcher. And he had apparently spread a rumour which she was being blamed for. How Mr Langley reached this conclusion she could not fathom. There must be more to the story than what he had told her. And this Spencer whom he'd spoken of before, he was Mr Langley's cousin? But in what way was he connected to her? It was all so mind boggling. And she certainly couldn't see how humiliating her, could possibly aid the wrongs done to his cousin and family.

She was confused. Nothing he'd said made any sense. Nothing except his final words, which spun round and around in her mind. 'I love you, Miss Dumont!' Could he be believed? 'I love you, Miss Dumont'. She harrumphed at the very notion If he loved her then he had the strangest way of showing it. Lying to her, abducting her, accusing her of wrongdoing.

Yet she could not forget the sweeter memories! He had saved her life twice. Firstly, from the fire, to which he'd tenderly administered to her burns. And then the day he took her riding across the Moor. He had been interesting, friendly and attentive during their ride, and she knew her feelings had grown substantially for him as they'd taken in the beauty of the land they rode. And then he'd saved her again, chased her as her horse spooked and ran and when she'd been thrown, he'd lifted her, cradled her against his heart; and although it was true that she'd been more than a little shocked to wake naked beside him, that feeling too quickly evaporated as he explained his actions. She respected the fact that he'd done his very best to save her life. Besides, how could one question or complain, his plan had worked, she was living proof of it.

She recalled his soft kisses. His hard kisses and the way his hands caressed her as he held her; how his fingers had danced awakening her skin to new, exciting sensations, how his delightfully wicked digit had worked her body…. No! she must not think such things, could not remember those feelings, it would only lead to madness. It seemed inconceivable, that she would never feel the tenderness of his touch again, she must put him in the past. Forget.

But as the carriage rolled on, her mind refused to give him up. She missed him. She was furious at him. She loved him! But he'd played with her. And there would be no going back. Therefore, she had no other choice than to continue her journey home. But four days, she would not bare it.

Tapping the roof of the carriage, and thrusting her hand out of the window, she waved her handkerchief to get Jackson's attention, then leaned from the carriage as the wheels started to slow and the carriage shuddered to a stop.

"Jackson," she called, "how much further to our first stop?"" She watched him dismount and walk stiffly, almost painfully to the door.

"I reckon maybe five hours, give or take to reach Plymouth, we'll be staying at the same Inn as afore, Miss," he said, wincing as he bent and straightened his knees to ease the ache.

"Well, that is where you can leave me and return home. I'll take the train the rest of the way," she declared.

Jackson looked shocked. "Are ye sure ye'd be safe Miss? I'm not sure the master would like me to leave ye on yer own."

"I'm quite certain the master wouldn't care, Jackson. He is after all, the one who wished for my speedy departure, and besides," she added gently. "It would save you the long journey in the cold. I'd be grateful if you'd arrange passage for me, once we arrive in Plymouth. Maybe for tomorrow?"

"I'll see what I can do, Miss, but the 'morrow is Christmas day, the train may already be full. But I'll do my best for ye."

Abigail closed the window and sat back in her seat with a deep sigh. This time tomorrow, all going well, she would be home, Mr Langley far away and she wondered how on earth she was going to explain her home coming to her father.

Darkness was drawing in as Jackson pulled the horses to a standstill and came to assist Abigail down the step. The solid ground beneath her feet seemed to sway, although she knew it was only her mind still dancing from the toing and froing of the carriage.

"I'm well," she said at Jackson's concerned gaze. "A little carriage drunk, that's all." His eyebrow rose at that, and her face lit with laughter, as she realized only hours ago, she had indeed been drunk in the carriage.

"I'll collect yer small trunk, while ye get yer land legs back," he said, "don't wander, there's a fair bit of drunken revelry going on, with it being Christmas Eve an' all."

He wasn't wrong, the noise assaulted her. Loud voices, stamping feet, bawdy singing came from within the Inn itself, and from the end of the street, she could hear the sea as it pounded its merciless beat against the sailing ships and rocky beach. The stench was almost overwhelming, the tangy scent of brine on the air, the smell of fish and the stink of urine in the streets. All of which had Abigail pining for the quiet darkness and fresh sweet air of the moor. She let out a quiet huff. She was missing the place that had given her nightmares, the place that she'd almost died, frozen for all time on Bodmin Moor. But right now, she craved its tranquil sounds, and understated beauty.

She knew she'd stood to long, when a grating voice accosted her ear and a hand grasped her arm, "ye're new 'ere 'ow about w …" the dirty hand gripping her was tugged away as Jackson hauled the man away. She watched in horror as the drunkard swung his fist and then gasped as Jackson, caught the balled hand in his own and twisted quickly, the man staggered, his arm now bent at an odd angle along his back, his head hung and Jackson reached out to grasp a handful of unruly hair and holding the man still, he spoke quietly into his ear. She couldn't hear what he said, but the moment he let go, the man stumbled forward and with a muttered curse he slipped away into the shadows.

"Ye alright, Miss?" Jackson asked as he picked up the case he'd dropped.

"I'm," she took a deep breath. "I'm astonished! He was so big, Jackson, and yet, how …" she stopped, her words falling over each other, how had this man, with some age to him, and almost half the size bested such a burly brute? And yet he had and with ease; "You are my hero, Jackson, thank you for saving me."

"Ahh, Lass. I've spent a lifetime breaking bigger beasts than that young colt. Did ye really think the Master would send ye away without protection? Come along now, it's freezing, let's get ye inside."

Once ensconced in the same room as she'd occupied on her previous journey, Abigail slumped into a chair and stared out of the window. Her journey was nearly at an end, tomorrow night she would sleep in her own bed. A week ago, that thought would have brought so much joy and now, a tear trickled down her cheek followed by another, and then she was sobbing, her head bowed low as she wept. Wept for the man who loved her too late; For the heart which lay cracked in her chest and cried tears of sadness to be leaving the place she wanted to call home.

She slept fitfully and was already waiting when Jackson knocked at her door at six the next morning. "Are ye ready, Miss? The train leaves in an hour," he said as she opened the door and helped him with her luggage.

The horses chuffed in the dark, cold air as she stroked down their long noses and smiled as one huffed into her hand, its long bristly, whiskers tickling her palm. She sighed, wondering if every time she stroked one of the large friendly beasts, she would think of the man who bred them? She walked to the door of the carriage and climbed inside. It seemed no time at all, before they pulled into the hustle and bustle of the busy railway station, and Jackson left her whilst he organised her trunk. On his return he opened her door, offering his hand which she gratefully grasped and stepped down, turning to face him as she did.

"Thank you, Jackson. I am grateful for all your assistance. I shall miss you."

"Ah, Miss, the house will feel yer loss. I am sorry that things didn't work out." He gave her a fond smile and took her gloved hand in his before adding, "it mightn't be my place to say, Miss, and I know the master's made a right mess of things, but he does love ye."

Abigail wiped away a tear. "And I loved him." A bell clanged and a loud voice yelled "All aboard" and people surged toward the opened door of the rail carriage. She clutched his arm, "Jackson, before I go, Mr Langley spoke of a man, it wasn't the first time he mentioned him. Spencer?"

"Spencer Ashcroft, Miss, his cousin and your…" A second bell cut through his words, "…tended?" He finished, as a burly fellow shoved past almost knocking Abigail off her feet. "Ye'd best hurry, Miss. 'Ere" he dug into his pocket and withdrew coins which he pressed into her palm. "Ye'll need some money for a hackney cab once ye disembark the train, and a little extra for ye, for work well done. Merry Christmas, Miss." He turned her before she had a chance to ask more and aided her up the steps and then with a wave, he walked away, disappearing into the crowd.

Abigail navigated to an empty seat and settled herself whilst glancing nervously around at her fellow passengers. A loud whistle pierced the air and with a jolt, the train pulled slowly away from the platform.

The train was no more comfortable a ride than Mr Langley's carriage. In fact, the seat on which she sat had far less cushioning than her conveyance from the day previous, and her buttocks ached, making her fidget. The train rocked, albeit not as much as the horse drawn carriage had, and the wheels made a lulling clickety clack sound in comparison to the crunching of stones, which, if her bottom hadn't been so sore, might have lured her into slumber with the monotony of it.

She thought instead, of Jackson's leaving comment. 'Mr Spencer Ashcroft, his cousin'. Could it be that Annabella's fiancé and Mr Langley's cousin were one and the same person? She could not recall Annabella referring to her fiancé by his full name, it was merely 'Mr Ashcroft did this, Mama,' or 'Mr Ashcroft did that'. There was no similarity what-so-ever between the two men. Mr Ashcroft, a high society gentleman in London, with light-brown curly hair, shorter than she herself in stature, and already sporting a slight paunch from too much drinking and society teas. Whereas Mr Langley, she pictured him astride his horse, his dark wind-blown hair, his face grave with the scar, not so much marring his perfection, but adding character, his heavily muscled arms and legs holding the large beast beneath him in check. A farmer, a horse-breeder, a bit of an out-cast but raised a gentleman non the less.

Was this then, the connection between his family and hers? She recalled Annabella's strange behaviour over the days before Abigail's departure. Had her sister been caught up in the lies? Was that what Father and Annabella's heated words had been about and the reason she had taken herself away to visit her aunt? The same night her father went to the gaming hall and drank himself into oblivion. The night he met Mr Langley. And if Mr Langley had indeed listened to the ramblings of the intoxicated man, then she could understand his anger, the betrayal he felt on behalf of his cousin, by none other than the family he was to marry into.

She closed her eyes at the thought of how very much he must have despised them. His planned revenge, in which to humiliate her family was born from the love he felt for his cousin. This to her dismay, she found honourable, and she could not hate him for that.

Chapter Thirty-Two

Edward groaned and clutched his head. His belly rumbled and he badly needed to relieve himself. He pulled the chamber from beneath the bed and unbuttoned his pants nearly freezing his balls off with the frigid temperature in the room. Once finished, he pushed the pot back under the bed and looked around the room. Remembered Miss Dumont had gone and buried his face back into the fading scent on her pillow and covered himself back up.

Chapter Thirty-Three

Jackson had watched the train pull away from the station before trudging back to the carriage, where the horses snorted at his arrival. He knew Edward wouldn't be expecting his return for another week and so decided to stay one more night at the Inn, giving the beautiful beasts a chance to rest for the day. That had been a mistake, for the following day the weather took a turn.

The journey home was downright miserable! The rain pelted down, stinging his face, for no matter how far down he set his cap, the almost horizontal rain caught his exposed skin. The horses were skittish, worried their bit and pulled on the rein. Well before he hit Wadebridge, the freezing rain turned to snow, and he shivered on the bench. Maybe he was getting too old for these long journeys during wintertime. The thought of a roaring fire spurred him on, and he coaxed the horses on with the promise of warm hay and oats. "Come on lads, we're almost home," he called, and urged them onward into the driving snow.

The house came into view and the sight of smoke rising from the chimneys warmed his heart. As he drove past the looming building toward the stables he was met by Tristan.

"*Alreet*, Mr Jackson, Sir, did ye have a good Christmastide? Me 'n Mam had a grand time."

"Ere it was a different one, lad. Can ye see to the horses, they've jest pulled down from Plymouth; they need a good rub down and feed," he chuckled and ruffled the lad's hair, "and I think I'm needing the same, tiz bleddy cold out."

And with that, Jackson headed out of the stables, back into the snow and trudged toward the house.

"Welcome home, Evelyn," he said, as he spotted the portly woman at the stove. Merry Christmas to ye." He shivered as he shook the snow from his cap, pulled his arms from the thick coat and toed off his boots.

"Aye, Christmas tidings to ye also. Where've yer been? Tiz bleddy cold out. Warm yerself, Jackson, and I'll fix ye a nice hot cuppa," she said as she bustled across the kitchen. "Where's the master too, is he not coming in with ye?" she asked putting leaves into the pot.

Jackson spun from warming his hands at the fire, "Ye've not seen 'im?"

"Naw, I've not seen 'im this mornin' an' our Teddy dropped us back at six. I assumed when 'e didn't come down, ye both had been about business, Tristan said the carriage were gone."

Jackson rushed from the kitchen, searching; poking his head round the study door, noted the roaring fire in the grate, but no Edward. He quickly moved to the dining room, again, the toasty warmth had him wanting to go and thaw his cold, aching body, but again, the room was empty. He turned and took the stairs two at a time running for the master's room. Knocked once, threw open the door. Cold and vacant! Panic filled him. What had the lad done, where was he?

He turned and eyed the closed door of Miss Dumont's room and suddenly he knew exactly where Edward was. He closed his eyes, took a deep breath, summoning his strength to deal with the broken man; he'd seen the young master through grief and loss before. Crossing to the room, he knocked softly and receiving no reply, turned the knob and pushed the door slowly open. The room was freezing, the curtains half drawn, letting in that blue-white brightness that only comes from a winter wonderland of snow and ice. Jackson's breath huffed out a hovering mist as he moved toward the bed, and pulling back the blanket uncovered the large, lumpy form of a man and was greeted by a loud grunting snore; loud even when muffled by the pillow that Edward had his face pressed into. Jackson shook his head and stepped around the bed to get a better look at the slumbering man, and let out a startled, painful curse as his stockinged foot landed on a jagged shard of broken bottle. He stumbled, tried to right himself but to no avail, and in slow motion he tumbled, landing on top of his young employer.

Chapter Thirty-Four

Edward startled awake, his fists coming up to fight off his would-be attacker, only to stop and stare, blurry eyed, at his Stable Manager.

"Jackson? What are you doing? Wait, you can't have delivered …" he stopped talking, hefted Jackson off him and jumped to his feet, he swayed as his head caught up with the movement, then turned to peruse the room. "Where is she? You brought her back."

He moved with urgency toward the open door, and then realizing how he must look and smell, in his sleep-worn wrinkled clothes, dirty boots still tied, although the mud had dried and crumbled away dirtying the white, cotton sheets, and the stench of alcohol foul on his breath. "I'll need to clean up, Jackson. What are you still doing sitting on the bed?"

"She's not here, lad! The young Miss is back home with her family."

"What? How? I have not slept for a week, Jackson, how did you…"

Jackson stood carefully, and limped back toward the door, "she caught the train from Plymouth," he interrupted, and cringed as he saw the look of horror on Edward's face; he knew how Edward hated the smelly, noisy contraptions. "She didn't wish to be travelling longer than she had to, and the train got 'er home for Christmas."

Edward glanced at the window, noting the thick white flurries fluttering against the glass, grimacing at its brightness and said, "but today is Christmas."

"No, lad. Yesterday was Christmas day."

Edward groaned and shook his head and moved back to sit on the edge of the bed. "She's really gone. I can't bear it, Jackson. I love her."

"Aye, I know lad," Jackson said softly, and hobbled over and placed a hand on the broken-hearted man. "And she loves ye as well, maybe ye should travel to London, see if ye can fix the mess ye've made."

"You're bleeding!" Edward said as if he'd not heard a word the older man had said noticing the red smears that Jackson's stockinged feet were leaving on the wooden floor. "Why are you bleeding?"

"Broken glass," the older man said wearily. "I think maybe one of the empty bottles got away from ye. I'll be right, once I've cleaned the wound."

"I'm so sorry," Edward said slowly silently berating himself for his temper tantrum which resulted in Jackson being cut. "Go, fix yourself. I'll deal with the mess, after all, I made it. Christ, they could put that line on my tomb stone."

Jackson limped out the door, closing it behind him. He didn't need Evelyn intruding on the young man's grief or of what remained of his pity party.

Edward lay back on the bed and brought the pillow to cover his face, breathing deeply and a small, quiet sob left his lungs when he realized her scent had gone, just as the woman it belonged to had gone.

Chapter Thirty-Five

Abigail's journey ended when the train ride, which had been barely six hours, pulled into the station. Her bottom screamed that she'd been sitting on the hard rocking seat for much, much longer.

It hadn't been difficult to hire a hackney cab to deliver her home, and Bernard, the butler, came out to relieve her of her luggage. "Welcome home, Miss Abigail, it's good to see you back."

"Thank you, Bernard, is my father in his study?"

"Yes, Miss, Mr Ashcroft has just departed, so I'm sure he'll be free to see you."

She walked into chaos. Her mother and sister calling for Bessie and Molly to assist with this and that, as they planned and strategized, the wedding it appeared, was back on. Abigail was disappointed that she'd missed Annabella's fiancé, but only because she wished to gain more information about his cousin, Mr Langley.

She found her father, as Bernard had said, in his study reading, quite unconcerned with all the shilly-shallying go on in the parlour, and he looked up in shocked surprise as she knocked at his door.

"Abigail?" um, welcome back, my dear," he said, putting his book face down on his desk and rose slightly from his chair as she placed a kiss on his lined face. "I didn't expect you," his voice caught, and he coughed onto the back of his hand, "I mean ..."

"I know what you meant, father." She pulled the two halves of the chit from the pocket of her coat and tore them into tiny pieces and taking his hand, placed them into his upturned hand. Her father stared in shock at the confetti littering is palm, and realized Abigail knew the truth, he turned his tormented, guilt-ridden eyes on her.

"Abigail, I was a fool. I am so, so sorry. I've barely slept since you went away. It was my stupidity which bought Mr Langley to our door. My debt; why the man could have taken everything from us, but the moment he saw you; he wanted nothing else. I'm afraid I took the easy way out; can you ever forgive me? I've prayed that he would be patient and kind with you. Oh, may the Lord strike me down, Abigail, if you've been hurt because,"

Abigail stopped him, a tremulous smile on her face. "There is no debt," she said, adding to herself, 'and there never was,' she could tell her father he'd done nothing wrong, that the debt was a ruse, but she didn't. Her father had sold her off to pay for his sins, if the signed chit had been for real, the outcome would have been the same. He had lied to her, led her to believe Mr Langley had come for her hand; and she decided in that moment, that her father and Mr Langley both were as guilty as each other. The pain she saw in her father's eyes now, was so like what she'd seen in Mr Langley's as she'd turned away from him in the carriage. Regret. Wishing to alleviate some of his pain, she smiled, "Mr Langley decided to forgo the debt and sent me home to surprise you all on Christmas day. Was that not kind of him?" she lied.

Her father looked at her expectantly. "Indeed, it was, my Dear. Will err Mr Langley be joining us too?"

"No, not today at least!" she said and then added, "it's possible he'll be here for the wedding. After all, he and Mr Ashcroft are related!"

"Really?" her father replied, his face paling slightly as he recalled the reason why he'd been drinking the night Mr Langley had found him. He'd been drowning his sorrows after his argument with Annabella, complaining bitterly to whomever would listen about his daughter having to break her engagement to the gentleman with such scandalous desires.

"Err, are they close in their relationship, or more like you and your cousin Maria, whom you don't get on well with at all?" he asked hopefully.

"No, father, Mr Langley is very loyal to his cousin, so much so, that he has been investigating rumours currently being circulated about him, and he has recently learned the identity of the scoundrel behind it all."

"He has? Well, that's wonderful news. Do we know this man, Abigail? Give me his name child." Her father could not hide the relief he felt, knowing the culprit could now be held accountable.

"He has been dealt with, I believe." She replied, "And I would not wish to speak out of turn, after all, that is how the rumour began in the first place. And I don't think you need worry yourself further; after all, the wedding is still going ahead, and Annabella seems happy again. Surely that is all that matters, is it not? "

"Yes, quite right," he said gruffly. "And what of yourself, Abigail, are you happy too? Mr Langley is a fine gentleman. I'm sure he will be eager for you to return to him after your sisters' nuptials?" he hedged, clearly wishing to discover how things stood between his youngest daughter and the man to whom he'd owed his fortune. "Tell me all. What of his residence?"

"He resides in Cornwall, Sir. A large property set on the outskirts of Bodmin Moor, and from my bed chamber I could look from my window and see the vast countryside."

Her father shuddered at the very thought, but his face brightened at the warmth of her tone. "Sounds charming," he said. "And err did his staff treat you well?"

Abigail thought of Jackson and the way he'd assisted her, coming to her rescue in Plymouth and smiled. "Oh yes, father, I was very well looked after." And then before he could continue to question her, she moved toward the door saying brightly, "I hope there is plenty of food left from dinner, I was too excited this morning to take breakfast, and there was no food served on the train; I wonder if that would be a suggestion you could pass to your acquaintances at your club, to supply nourishment during a journey. I'm quite sure it could be lucrative." Her father stared at her in astonishment. "Father don't look so surprised; woman can have ideas you know; you must have noticed that I read all the time; surely you didn't think it was Mama who steals your newspapers?" She smiled at him. And while he was pondering her question, she quietly took her leave.

Her mother greeted her with a stiff hug and a searching look which Abigail could not quite decipher, "Has Mr Langley accompanied you home?" She asked.

"No, Mama, he is still in Cornwall. I travelled by carriage to Plymouth and from there, by train, I so wished to spend Christmas with my family," she continued with the white lie she'd told her father.

"Alone? You travelled alone? What was Mr Langley thinking?" her mother's voice had risen, and both Abigail and Annabella stared in surprise at her volume.

"Yes, Mama, alone! I seem to recall you having no qualms of my travelling down to Cornwall in such a manner. Surely my sitting in a train filled with passengers for half a day was much safer than a four-day journey by road," she replied not quite able to keep the sarcasm from her voice.

Her mother looked like she'd swallowed a lemon, her eyes widening in disbelief that her youngest daughter would use such a tone with her.

Annabella smiled at her, "come on," she said and tugged her young sister's hand, "let's go and find you some dinner and you can tell me all about your train trip." Abigail had no choice, but to be pulled along, although she wondered why Annabella sought her company, they'd barely spoken since Annabella came out at the beginning of the season.

Her mother screeched behind them, "Annabella, you've no time to waste, we have much to do for your wedding. Besides, I'm sure Abigail can find her way to the kitchen, alone," she emphasized the word giving her youngest a wide-eyed glare.

"I won't be long, Mama," Annabella called over her shoulder as she pulled Abigail through the door, and they headed toward the kitchen.

Abigail almost wept. The kitchen as usual was warm and welcoming, and Bessie rushed to her, enveloping her tightly into a loving embrace as she sniffed and wiped her tears on the younger woman's shoulder.

"Welcome back, Miss Abigail," she whispered.

"Bessie, Miss Abigail needs some food, she's not eaten all day." Annabella said, and Abigail cocked her head, she'd told her father that, had Annabella been listening?

Once Bessie had shuffled away, Annabella caught her eye, "Now, tell me what you know about these rumours." She demanded.

So, she had been eves dropping. Abigail pulled a chair from the table and sat, wincing at the sting as her buttocks touched the wooden seat, and Annabella sat opposite, leaning her elbows on the table like a young child as Abigail recited what she'd told her father, again, excluding the name of the rumourmonger and barely touching on the reason for her departure to Cornwall, and omitted her reason for leaving completely. She couldn't tell her sister the truth, to do so would incriminate Mr Langley in his breach of etiquette, and her own. No, she would not tarnish the name of the man she loved no matter how painfully he'd broken her heart. "Now you," she said, "will you tell me what happened that day? And what Mr Ashcroft did for you to forgive him?"

Annabella flushed. "I didn't have anything to forgive, Abbey, Mr Ashcroft really didn't do anything wrong." She smiled at the confused look on her sister's face, 'I'll start at the beginning."

"I broke 'the' rules, Abbey!"

Abigail's face warmed, yes, Mama's rules, they were laughable, especially since Abigail herself had broken every single one in the last week. She'd drunk alcohol, she'd been alone with a man, and she'd give herself up to a man's touch.

Abigail pushed her memories away and listened as Annabella told her story. "Mama and I attended one of Lady Devonish's famous soirees. There were so many people attending, the rooms were overly hot and stuffy and I found myself sipping punch as I waited for Mr Ashcroft to arrive; I feel I may have over imbibed which is possibly why I didn't hesitate when Mr Ashcroft took my hand as if to dance, but then escorted me from the ballroom without Mama seeing, and with no chaperone to stop him, he kissed me! It was wonderful, oh Abbey I can't find the words to describe it. I knew it was wrong, and I knew Mama would be searching ..." The hot flush that burned her cheeks inched down her neck and mottled the skin on her chest as she continued to whisper "...but it was so lovely, and I didn't want to stop. After all, I told myself, we were engaged to be married, surely Mama's rules didn't apply between people who are betrothed, and then, Abbey, you shall think me scandalous, for Mr Ashcroft lifted my skirts, and I not only allowed it, but assisted." A fortnight ago, Abigail most certainly would have been mortified at her sister's behaviour, but now, after she'd felt the wonder of Mr Langley's hand on her skin, there was more a air of camaraderie in the look she gave Annabella, nodding for her to continue.

"I thought us to be alone in our passions, so what a fright I had when Lord Dandion appeared behind Mr Ashcroft startling him terribly with a hand to his shoulder. Mr Ashcroft still held me, I suppose to shelter my state of undress, but I was so embarrassed that I abruptly pushed him away; panicking because we'd been discovered, and agitated that my fiancé had, um, almost... well never mind that; I was upset that he hadn't immediately ordered Lord Dandion to leave and I said some terrible things before I ran, pulling down my skirts, whilst Mr Ashcroft chased me in a state of undress, and Lord Dandion smiling as if it was the best entertainment ever bringing up the rear . I came home that night determined to call of my wedding. A couple of days later, Molly, in our very own kitchen, told me she'd heard a rumour confirming my fears, that my fiancé and Lord Dandion were, well, involved.

Mr Ashcroft called on me the following day, but I refused to receive him, and father was none too pleased that he had to send him on his way. Mama took me to stay with our aunt to give me time to address my broken heart. And when I got back, you were gone, and father was beside himself."

"I'm sure he was," Abigail said.

"Anyway," she continued as if Abigail hadn't spoken. "Mr Ashcroft was concerned I would break our engagement and took it upon himself to discover who the scandalmonger was. So determined was he, that he visited Lord Dandion himself.

And now I get to why I've reconsidered. I received a letter from the Lord himself with his heart-felt apologies and an explanation as to how he came to be in the library that night." She withdrew a folded page tucked into the neckline of her gown and unfolding it, she began to read.

"Dear Miss Dumont

I wish to offer you a heartfelt apology for the circumstances of our introduction. I am aggrieved that you were dragged into my personal affairs. As both yours, and Mr Ashcroft's happiness is in jeopardy, I feel impelled to write.

My rendezvous point was the study, directly across from the library. I was detained by Lady Devonish, so sent word to 'my friend' via a maid.

I arrived to discover, to my dismay, my lover with not one, but two maids. Needing a moment, I entered the library seeking solitude.

"So, you see, once I'd received the letter, I sent one of my own to Mr Ashcroft requesting that he call, and it was decided we would continue with our plans as before."

"Annabella!" Their mother's angry voice rang through the house.

"I'd best go help, Mama," she said and rose from her seat and hurried from the kitchen.

Bessie placed a plate of roasted meat and potatoes in front of her and Abigail picked at the food, finding she wasn't as hungry as she thought. Bessie sat with her and listened proudly, as Abigail told how she had cooked whilst staying in Cornwall, recounting what she'd made and how she'd thought of the little woman in front of her, each time she'd been in the kitchen.

She made her excuses early, pleading a headache and escaped to her room, crawling between the sheets, in the room she'd slept in since she was a child. She took a deep breath, then let it out with a loud sigh. Shook loose the tense muscles in her shoulders and neck, then closed her eyes, praying for the oblivion of sleep to take her, to give her peace from her thoughts, thoughts of him.

For so many years this room had been her haven, yet now she discovered that she missed her big room in Cornwall; she missed the fullness of the mattress, the down-filled pillows; she missed the roaring flames in the fireplace, the way they lit her room, bathing it in a glorious orange glow, the logs crackling and spitting, holding at bay the pitch dark, and quiet of the Cornish night.

Outside the house, Christmas revellers were loud. Men with their bellies full of spirits streamed from the neighbouring houses, some heading home and others too drunk to know where they were going. Abigail could not fall sleep. She turned this way and that and finally lay flat on her back, the covers up to her chin and stared at the ceiling lit by the streetlights that had yet to be extinguished. Her mind scrolling once more through all the information she had gleaned in the last two days. Mr Langley's words made much more sense after hearing her sister's sorry story, and Abigail recognized that her anger, her animosity toward him had disappeared. He must have been so very vexed for his cousin, worried about his family over such terrible slander. She wondered how he was coping with the news that Mr Fletcher, his good friend, was the cause of so much pain and then there was the discovery of his affair with Lord Dandion.

Finally with drooping eyelids, the blankets pulled tight around her ears, her mind conjured the image of a large, handsome man, astride his sturdy black horse, riding hell bent toward her, and she smiled, as sleep finally pulled her under.

Chapter Thirty-Six

"Mornin' Sir," Evelyn greeted, when Edward finally stepped into the kitchen. "Can I get ye something to break yer fast?"

"Just coffee I think, Evelyn, and welcome home, I trust you had a good time with your sister?" he responded, voice gravelly.

"Aye, t'was lovely to see her, Sir. I'll bring yer coffee through, and I've left yer correspondence on yer desk. Picked it up on me way through the village."

"Thank you, Evelyn," Edward muttered, and turned and strode out of the kitchen toward his study, where he sat with a thump and let his head slump forward to the blotter on the desktop. He felt like death, the beat in his temples drummed louder than the damaged muscle in his chest. He jumped when Evelyn set a steaming mug beside him and croaked out "thank you," without lifting his head and he listened as she shuffled out of the room and closed the door behind her.

The coffee's strong aroma dragged his head up and he gratefully took a sip of the steaming elixir, cradling the cup to his chest as he collapsed back into his chair. He hadn't felt this lost since the day he'd buried his father, when he'd come and sat in this very seat after the funeral; the seat which had always belonged to his Father and mentor; the man who had survived so much and had always seemed so strong. What would he think of his son if he could see him right now? Would he be proud of the way he ran his business? Maybe. Would he be proud of his behaviour over the past few days? Hell No!

An envelope with bold cursive caught his eye. He would know Spencer's penmanship anywhere. He set the mug back on the desk and picked up the envelope, slipping the letter opener at the seal he sliced the paper in one clean swipe and pulled out not one but two folded sheets of paper. Opening the first, he sat forward, leaning his elbows on his desk and began to read.

Edward

Where to begin?

When last we met four weeks ago, can you believe it was only four weeks? It feels like a lifetime. My situation, you will happily learn, has vastly improved.

I wallowed for some days when you left, unwilling to venture out and face the embarrassment and shame of it all. Anger and self-pity would have consumed me if it weren't for the very real despair I felt, not knowing if I'd lost the love of my darling, Miss Dumont.

Each day that past was both a curse and a relief, as each night I bedded down not knowing which path my fiancé would take, to forgive or to break our engagement.

I decided to follow your advice and discover the voice behind the lies and so took it upon myself to visit Lord Dandion; considering he too was a recipient in the derogatory rumour.

I'm delighted to say, Lord Dandion, or rather, Julian, as he has insisted on being called, was extremely apologetic for the ruination of Miss Dumont and my tête-à-tête and the awkwardness which followed. His explanation of why he approached, simple, he wished to make his presence in the library known to us as we, in our impassioned state had failed to notice him. It appears his own rendezvous in the study opposite had not gone as planned which left him feeling disheartened and he'd sought the dark, quiet room in which to ruminate on seeing his lover with not one, but two serving girls.

Edward did a double take at that, his lover with two serving girls; Francis, the lover was Francis. Francis and Julian Dandion were lovers! God, he'd known his friend had someone in town but... His eyes re-skimmed that part of the letter and he shook his head, no, he had not seen that coming.

The letter continued:

Julian is certain his, now former, lover noted our trio's not-so-subtle exit and viciously spread the lies. Try as I might, he would not name the culprit, but to assist with my courtship, wrote a missive to Miss Dumont to which I added my own apology and declaration of love.

The final banns were read last Sunday, and an invitation to visit at the Dumont residence has me hoping Miss Dumont means to go forth with our betrothal. I shall call at her father's house on Christmas Day to, God-willing, cement our coming union and as such, have attached with this letter an invitation to the wedding, for the first Sunday after Christmas.

It seems all is bright and right with the world once more, and once my vows to Miss Dumont in the eyes of the church are complete, the scandalous rumours will be forgotten.

I look forward to seeing you

Spencer.

Edward dropped the pages to the desk and pulled open the folded invitation, his eyes drifting across the words.

Mr and Mrs Gordon Dumont

Request the honour of your presence

At the marriage of their daughter

Annabella Isabel

To

Mr Spencer James Ashcroft

Sunday, December Thirty-one,

Eighteen Hundred and Ninety-Five

At Eleven o'clock in the morning

St James Church

Sussex Gardens

Paddington

Each word an arrow to his chest, and then because he could not bear it, he reached for his scribe and crossed out his cousin's name and wrote 'Edward Langley' in his place. Then he crushed the paper in his fist and slumped back in his chair. Miss Dumont was to be married in five days' time. His coffee went cold, and the roaring fire turned to embers, but it didn't matter. Nothing mattered.

The wintery day quickly darkened to night and still Edward sat. Jackson and Evelyn both, had knocked at his door and left again when there was no response.

Snow piled up against the house and the world was silent, the darkness outside was no different to how he felt inside himself. How had everything gone so horribly wrong? His Miss Dumont was to be Mrs Ashcroft, and the mere thought of Spencer touching her had him seething, yet he had no right, none whatsoever. She would be his cousin's wife, and Edward would either learn to live with it, or he would cut his ties with his cousin and live like a hermit here

in Cornwall, very like he had after his face was carved. He'd
hidden then for self-preservation, he damn well could again.

Sometime in the early hours of the morning,
exhausted, cold and aching, he climbed the stairs and
trudged down the hallway, bypassing his bedroom and
entered Miss Dumont's room; only it wasn't her room
anymore, she left. 'On your command', the nagging voice in
his head reminded. He curled himself onto the bed, dragged
the blankets up and over his head and slept.

Chapter Thirty-Seven

Abigail stirred as a knock sounded at her door and before she had the chance to answer, her sister bowled into the room, climbed uninvited into bed and pulled the covers around her.

"It's absolutely freezing," Annabella shivered, snuggling up to her younger sister, pressing her cold feet against Abigails toasty warm ones and making her squeal.

"Where are your slippers?" Abigail asked, dragging her legs further across the bed and away from the icebergs as Annabella tried to get closer to steal her warmth. "What time is it?"

"Early," Annabella answered. "It might be the only time I get you to myself. Mama is entirely engrossed in the wedding plans and expects me to be the same. And besides, yesterday in the kitchen, don't think I didn't notice that you left out all the details about you and your Mr Langley."

"He isn't my, Mr Langley," Abigail answered and quickly turned her face to the window to hide the welling tears. Annabella saw and with a gentle hand on her chin, turned her back so she could see her face.

"But you want him to be?" she guessed. "What happened?"

Abigail sniffled and raising Annabella's arm, pulled it around her shoulders, snuggling into her side.

"Mr Langley didn't want me. I was merely a pawn in which to seek his vengeance. He believed I was behind the gossip which had spread about his cousin and wished for me and my family to feel the sting of humiliation as his family had."

"That makes no sense, Abbey. Why would he think you'd do such a thing? Surely, he must realize, that the rumour was as devastating to your own sister as to Mr Ashcroft. You would never hurt me that way." Abigail gave her sister a tight hug and then moved away, settling herself against the headrest and hauling the blankets up and over them both.

"Why he'd believe it, is a mystery to me." Abigail said sadly.

"You still have feelings for this man, Abbey. If he was trying to humiliate you, I'm guessing he failed, or didn't try hard enough if you have fallen for him."

"Well, that's the thing. As angry as he appeared on the night I arrived, he wasn't unkind, just a bit gruff and he frowned a lot. He was watchful, almost wary, as if readying himself for a battle.

I burned myself that night, and he rescued me; he literally wrapped his arm around my waist, lifting me off my feet," she grew quiet as she remembered the feeling of that strong arm as it banded her body, hauling her from the flames to be held against him.

"And?" Annabella nudged her, "what did he do then?"

"I don't recall. I fainted dead away and when I came to, I was on the dining room table," she giggled as Annabella's eyes rounded.

"He put you on the table. Oh, Abbey, that is so, so," she fanned her face with her hand and they both laughed.

"My gown had caught fire, and he had ripped away the burning material and administered to my wounds. He was gentle, tentative and I believe that was when I first began to feel something for the man. But I fought my feelings, told myself how much I hated him."

"Could the maids not have seen to your wounds?" Annabella mused. Abigail's face flamed red. "What, Abbey, what aren't you telling me?"

"You must promise, Annabella, that you will never tell Father or Mama, what I am about to tell you." Abigail crooked her little pinky finger towards her sister, who frowned but quickly hooked it with her own, just as they had done when they were children.

"I swear to keep your secret," she said solemnly.

"I was taken there to be Mr Langley's servant and not for us to wed as Father intimated. That was, I believe, how Mr Langley meant to humiliate me, by having me work as an unpaid maid. Other than Jackson, that's Mr Langley's Stable Manager, I was alone with Mr Langley."

"No Abbey, that can't be true. No gentleman would allow such a thing," Annabella gasped

"It's the truth."

"So, you cooked and cleaned for him; he did not take anything more from you?" her sister gave her that knowing look and Abigail's chest squeezed tight.

"No, he didn't *take* anything. But." she stopped, thinking back, he had initiated those kisses, and she hadn't fought him, in fact, she'd responded.

"But?" Annabella prompted. "Something did happen, didn't it?"

"We were having a heated discussion and, well, he kissed me." She said very quickly and turned her body toward her sister. "He kissed me, and it was wonderful."

"That was all?" she pushed.

"Yes, that time. An acquaintance of Mr Langley discovered us, and I fled the room."

"Someone else saw you. I thought you said there were only the three of you," her sister said.

"The man wasn't meant to come to the house. Mr Langley had arranged to meet him at the stables, he was buying a horse, you see. I'm quite sure Mr Langley wouldn't have mentioned my name."

"And this was the only time you saw him, the buyer, that is," Annabella question, her face in a grim mask. "Rumours can be spread very fast, Abigail. I should know."

"Well, no. I saw him briefly one more time, but never to converse with. I believe he really did think that I was the maid."

"I still can't believe Mr Langley would put you in such a position; it is hard to believe he is related to Mr Ashcroft," she stated.

"Oh really?" Abigail gaped at her sister. "Have you forgotten the story you told only yesterday where your fiancé whisked you away unchaperoned, got caught with his pants down and was the reason why I was in that predicament to begin with?"

Annabella bit her lip to stop herself laughing, but it was no good, she grabbed her little sister, and they chortled together.

"I'm sorry," Annabella gulped, trying to hold back the giggles. "Please, finish your story, before Mama comes screeching for me."

"Well, he kissed me again, ran his finger up my arms, touched my neck," goosebumps rose on her arms and her fingers stroked at her throat as she spoke, "and then withdrew into himself as if he'd done something wrong; it felt like every time we started to get close, something got in the way. I did wonder if there was someone else on his mind, someone keeping him from taking what he wanted. What I wanted him to take. You know?"

Annabella nodded, oh yes, she knew those feelings. "So why did you leave?"

"He sent me away. He, we, well, he pleasured me, just his fingers," she added quickly when Annabella gasped. "But I wanted more, and I let him know that I wanted more," Abigail said truthfully. "And he walked away. The next morning he'd ordered the coach, and I left. It was devastating leaving, thinking I would never see him again. But I did see him again, he chased after me, the man I was so very in love with, tracked us down and for a moment my hopes soared, thinking he'd changed his mind, that he wanted me after all. But it was not to be. He came to unburden himself. And to tell me he'd discovered I was innocent after all, that he'd found the rumourmonger. It was at this time that he also disclosed the truth about wishing to humiliate me." Annabella took her hand and gave it a gentle squeeze. "My heart cracked. I broke when I thought all our intimacies were simply him teaching me a lesson in humiliation, and I threw him out. Refused to listen to his explanations. And as we drove away, I could hear him pleading for me not to go and shouting that he loved me."

"Abbey, poor, poor Abbey, what a trial you've been through. And poor Mr Langley." Annabella sympathised.

Abigail's head shot up, "What? Poor Mr Langley, why?"

"Don't you see, Abbey. He is most probably drowning his sorrows as we speak. To have declared his love for you, and you rode away. I'm not defending his actions, his intentions in his silly scheme, but I can see how you are feeling, how broken you are at losing the person who means the world to you, and, well, hasn't he just lost the same if he is as much in love with you, as you are with him?"

"Annabella, Annabella, where are you," their mother's voice came from down the hall.

"Coming, Mama." Annabella called back, and quickly engulfing Abigail in a tight hug, she released her and climbed from the bed, exiting the room and leaving Abigail with her thoughts.

<u>**Chapter Thirty-Eight**</u>

Snowflakes fell. Silent as a thief it stole the landscape, hiding landmarks beneath its blanket of blinding white.

Edward stared from his window, sober and impatient. If he were to stop Miss Dumont marrying his cousin, it meant he would need to leave tomorrow, that is, if he could find the damned road beneath the white fluff that was still falling, thick and fast.

A thud sounded and his study door opened. Jackson pushed his way in using his shoulder, his arms filled with logs that had melting snow dripping on the rug. "Tiz a right white-out," he grumbled as he knelt and deftly unloaded the logs into the wood bin.

"We're leaving for London tomorrow!" Edward stated. "Spencer is to marry Miss Dumont on Sunday. I cannot allow her to marry him without her knowing my true feelings."

"It will be a cold, hard ride, Sir." Jackson said, straightening from his crouched position by the fire. "For you and the horse."

"That's why we'll go by carriage. You and I can share the driving, giving each other a break from the cold, and we can hire a new team at each stop." He'd thought this over whilst staring at the blank, white canvas outside. "We'll leave at first light and just pray the snow stops."

The following morning, after leaving instruction for Tristan to keep the stables cleaned, horses fed and the ice knocked off the water troughs, Jackson stacked blankets and stowed away the basket of food from Evelyn, readying the carriage. The horses wore warm covers beneath their harness; this would be a slow trip, no over exertion to cause them to overheat, just a casual, steady plod. He pulled the carriage to a stop in front of the large house and Mr Langley strode down the steps, bag in hand. He moved to the horses, watching as their hooves pawed at the snow, prancing a little as the cold fluff swirled and settled just below their knees.

"I'll take first shift," Jackson said, pulling his cap low to shield his eyes; climbing onto the bench and covering his legs with an old horse blanket then waited whilst Edward settled himself and shut the door. Edward's prayer had been answered, and the snow had stopped sometime in the night, but the pinkish cloud as far as the eye could see was foreboding, there was to be another dumping, and he only hoped they were well on their way before those clouds released their load.

Two hours later, and not too many miles beneath their belts, Jackson pulled on the rein, and the horses came to a standstill. Stomping a little, they lifted their heads, scenting the cold air like they knew the next snow fall was imminent and they were more than ready to move so as not to be caught in it. Jackson climbed stiffly from the bench and hobbled to the door. They had decided that two hourly stints would be more than enough time sitting in the frigid air. Edward pulled his coat collar up tightly round his ears, and smoothed the leather gloves onto his fingers, climbed from the carriage he nodded at the red-faced, watery-eyed man as they passed one another, and Edward took up the reins. Driving was hard going; especially when the road widened without trees or shrubbery at either side, it would be far too easy to stray from the beaten track. The concentration it took was exhausting; add to that the biting cold of the wind and the glare from the snow and Edward found his eyes watering and a headache forming at his temples.

Edward was pleased to note the snow wasn't so dense the second time he took up the reins. His fingers had taken almost all of his two hours back in the carriage to thaw and unstiffen. The road was easier to see, and the horses were able to pick up the pace from a slow plod to a decent trot. Time dragged. And by the time he took the reins for the third time, dusk was beginning to creep over the countryside, but in the gloom, he was able to make out the lights of Plymouth, his aching face stretched into a smile, so pleased to see civilization, his body relaxed, and he cajoled the horses onward. The end of the first leg was in sight.

He pulled the carriage to a stop at the stables and a groom rushed to aid him and Jackson to unhitch his team. Unlike most gentlemen, Edward was hands on when it came to caring for his beloved horses and found to his delight that rubbing the large animals down, helped to bring movement back into his own aching muscles and by the time they left the stables he was smiling as he exchanged pleasantries with those around him.

The Inn was quiet, and Edward took little time in chartering two rooms with orders of hot water for bathing.

The second day dragged like the first, although the snow wasn't thick, the road was icy. The wind stung any exposed skin, and the cold air burned in their lungs. The hired horses were of good breeding stock and made decent time as they crunched over the stoney road towards their next stop in Exeter.

Day three started like the two previous, there was little snow now, but the bitter wind howled around them and by midmorning the rain sheeted horizontally into their faces. As the two exchanged places, Jackson coughed, dragged in a rattling breath and coughed again. "Get inside, man," Edward growled, and watched as the old man climbed wearily into the carriage and covered himself with the blankets. Edward shut the door and climbed onto the wet wooden bench, his coat and hat already dripping. He could hear Jackson coughing as he flicked the reins and urged the horses forward as fast as they would go. He didn't stop once his two hours were up, he pushed on, and a little over an hour later was gratified to see the lights of Bristol through the driving rain. As other nights, Edward attended the horses and arranged for their rooms and a bath. But Jackson, his cough a dry hack and his nose dripping had been sent by his master, straight to his room. Edward knocked at Jackson's door a few hours later, once he'd thawed out in his own bath and eaten a large helping of hearty, beef stew. The coughing sounded through the door and Edward called out that he was coming in. What he found made his heart drop, Jackson was abed, sweat dripping as he shivered under the blankets, his chest heaving as he fought to regain his breath from his latest bout of coughing. "Jackson, you sound terrible." he said. "I shall call for a physician immediately."

The prognosis for their continued journey the next day was not good. In fact, Edward barely used the room he'd rented for himself, preferring to stay near Jackson and administer the potion which had been bought in from the apothecary; it smelled disgusting, and Jackson shuddered every time Edward pushed the spoon between his lips with the foul-tasting medicine.   Jackson's fever broke late on their second night, and he finally slept. Edward dozed in the chair and woke in the early hours, neck stiff and his eyes burning, badly in need of a good night's sleep himself, but there was no time. "Ye've got to go, lad. Leave me and the carriage, a horse will be faster on its own," he coughed and then said, "unless ye want to take the train?" and smirked at Edwards reaction. "Horse tiz then. Go, I'll follow soon as I'm able." Jackson was right, he had to go and go now.

The day was arduous. The weather had improved, the rain stopped, but it didn't make the ride any less harrowing. Edward had run an appreciative eye over the horses that morning, choosing a large, black with expressive eyes, and prancing feet, he was ready to run. He'd given the beast his head as soon as they found the open road and the horse took him swiftly away from bustling Bristol to the cold, empty countryside. But not for too long, he'd reigned him in, not wishing for him to weary himself too quickly. The day dragged, and it was gone dark before he saw the lights of Reading; his last stop before reaching London. Another stable, another Inn, another bed and he slept like a babe.

The next morning, he rose and was back in the saddle before dawn lit the sky with heavy pinkish clouds, and Edward groaned at the thought of more snow. He didn't have time to slow down, Miss Dumont would be marrying his cousin today if he didn't reach the church by eleven. He urged his mount onward, faster and wondered for the umpteenth time how to approach Miss Dumont and how she would receive him. No matter, he'd come this far, he would not be deterred. If she didn't want him, then he would back away, he wouldn't like it, not one bit, but her happiness was more important to him than his own.

The snow began to drift down as he gained the outskirts of London, and he slowed his mount to a walk and pulled out his pocket-watch again, frowning at the damned hands which would not slow down, no matter how much he wished.

<u>**Chapter Thirty-Nine**</u>

The week had flown by. Abigail had barely had time to think let alone dwell on her broken heart. She'd been thrust feet first, into wedding strategies, first task; a gown. She'd barely finished dressing her first morning home when there came a tapping on her bedroom door and Molly who usually worked beside Bessie in the kitchen, had requested Abigail follow her to the parlour, where awaiting her, a seamstress with a rail of dresses and bolts of fabric.

"Come, Abigail. Make haste," her mother grumbled at her. "We must find you something to wear. Annabella wishes you to be her witness and there is nothing in your armoire that is, well, let us just say, not correct for standing up at a wedding."

"Surely, Mama, one of my ballgowns could be altered slightly, or even my …"

"No, I'll not have it said, you've not been dressed appropriately," her mother interrupted. "Now the seamstress has kindly brought some gowns to try; behind the screen girl, we'll try this one first Ms Forester," she said pointing to a bright yellow gown which took up half the space on the rack, the skirt was so wide.

"No, Mama," Abigail had said instantly. "What we want is something that will not outshine the bride, something tasteful, elegant to be sure, but simple, yes! Something simple. That one in the middle Ms Forester," she said, "no, to the left, next one. That's it!" She turned and walked behind the screen as Ms Forester, without so much as a glance at Mrs Dumont followed and assisted with the removal of her day gown and held the blue satin dress for her to step into. The cool material caressed her thighs, her hips, as the seamstress pulled it up over her body, tightening the laces at the back and fluffing out the tops of the Juliette sleeves. She moved in front of Abigail, a furtive glance to check her breasts were concealed by the Queen Anne neckline, then leaning forward, she tweaked the long, flowing skirt, just once, and then took Abigails hand, lifted it above her head and twirled her. The skirt billowed slightly, then settled, just like wine settles to the bottom of the glass after being swirled. Abigail loved it. "This is the style, Ms Forester, now if I may see the fabrics?"

"Certainly, Miss Dumont, I'll just assist," she pursed her lips as she undid the laces and tugged it gently down, "there," she said and taking the gown moved away, replacing it back on the rack.

"Abigail, surely you cannot be happy with the first gown you try," her Mama complained.

"Like I said, Mama. I wished for something elegant and simple, there are no bows, no buttons, no frills, it is perfect. It took a while longer for her to decide on a colour, the swatches the seamstress held out to her were not to her liking, although her mother pointed and commented on how very well each would look. And then she saw what she was after. A bolt of silvery-grey satin. She sighed when she saw it, taken back to the Moor, her dream where the mist had moved like this very bolt of fabric, and she wondered at Mr Langley's reaction to her wearing the mist that encompassed his property.

"I like this one," she stated, ignoring her Mama's tightening lips. She stood and made her way toward the door.

"Where are you going?" Mama called, "you've yet to be measured and …"

"Ms Forester, if you'd please, make the gown to the exact measurements to the one you just fitted." Abigail called over her shoulder, "and I'm more than happy to visit you for the final fitting." And with that, Abigail, ignoring her mother's angry glare, opened the door and she was free.

Abigail found her feet taking her where they always had when she wanted comfort and love. She pushed the kitchen door open and instantly felt the warmth that was Bessie.

"You've finished already? I thought with so many clothes that Ms Forester pushed through, that you'd be there all day," Bessie said giving Abigail a warm hug.

"I knew what I was wanting, and besides, we don't have the time, poor Ms Forester fingers will be sore enough having to make double the dresses now that I'm back. I am more than happy to wear something simple, no frills. Besides, it's Annabella's day, not mine," she finished and then stilled as she heard her own words. *Not mine*.

She gave Bessie a woeful look, touching her fingers to her eyes to hold back the moisture forming. "I'm in love with Mr Langley, Bessie!" she stated.

Bessie took her hand and moved them both to the table, "You sit there, and I'll get some tea," she said moving around the spotlessly clean kitchen, "then you can tell me all about it."

As Abigail sipped at the sweet tea, she confided her hopes and thoughts to the woman whom she vehemently wished had been her real mother; she could never have had this discussion with Mama, with her judgement and overbearing rules. The woman who had intentionally sent her youngest daughter, with no chaperone to protect her reputation, to sleep beneath the roof of a man they barely knew.

"I miss him, Bessie. And I miss the house and Jackson. I don't know how to tell Father and Mama that there is to be no wedding. That Mr Langley sent me away."

"Well, my love, I think that is something we keep between us until after your sister is wed, after all, your Mr Langley may come to the wedding and try to win you back," she said, a soft smile on her lips, "how could he not fall in love with you?"

"But that's just it, Bessie. He said he did love me, and the kisses and the touches felt like heaven, except he acted differently afterward, like he'd stolen something that wasn't his, like my kisses weren't meant for him. Does he not deem himself worthy because of his appearance? His business? Is that why he laughed at the very idea of marrying me? I don't understand!" she said folding her arms on the table and burying her face in them, while Bessie rubbed her back, soothingly.

"The only way to stop you from overthinking is to keep you busy," Bessie said, "I've got far too much to do for this wedding menu your mother has decided on and an extra pair of hands would be helpful." Abigail unbuttoned her cuffs and rolled her sleeves back and smiled at her favourite person.

Bessie made good on her word, with all the preparations there was barely time to think and when she wasn't helping in the kitchen, she was at Ms Foresters establishment for her dress fittings, or she was flitting around after Annabella who suddenly seemed unable to decide anything on her own. What flowers to carry? What veil to choose? Hair pins, bows, clips; Abigail had sat for hours going through Annabella's accessories with her.

Before she knew it, Saturday evening was upon them, and the house seemed quiet after the rushing, the toing and froing of the past week as the preparations wound down and with nothing more to be ticked from her mother's list. Abigail let out a long sigh and relaxed for the first time since coming home. She looked at the beautiful dress which hung from her dressing screen in the corner, the silvery mist swirled each time somebody opened her door, and she wondered how Mr Langley would perceive her choice, would he recognise the resemblance to the moor outside his doors? Would he grasp that she'd been thinking of him as she chose? Was he here? Had he caught the train from Plymouth? Was he right this very minute somewhere in London, with his cousin maybe, toasting to the upcoming wedding? The thought made her giddy, he could be so close, she moved to the window, as if glancing out she could catch sight of him; there was nobody out on the street, the cold had seen to that, nobody in their right mind would be out in this weather.

Abigail slept fitfully; her stomach churned as her nerves danced a jig at the mere prospect of being in the same space as Mr Langley. She rose early and joined Bessie in the kitchen where she drank a cup of tea and nibbled on a biscuit, trying to settle herself.

"Will he be there?" Bessie asked

"I cannot see reason why he would not be, unless he does not wish to see me," Abigail replied ruefully.

"Nobody would wish that," Bessie assured her. "Then again, if he was to see you right now, sitting in your housecoat, well," she gave a cheeky grin. "Go on with you, best get upstairs and see if Miss Annabella needs you."

She climbed the stairs and knocked on her sister's door and entered. Annabella had finished washing and was being helped into her underclothes by Molly. While Trudy, Mrs Dumont's maid was waiting patiently by the walnut vanity, grouping pins and clips, readying them for Annabella's hair.

"Good morning, Abbey, have you come to join my party? You could have Trudy do your hair while I finish here," her sister said, "Go on, sit, have you decided on a style?"

Abigail sat and took up her sister's brush and pulled it through the long waves, "well, I had thought a simple roll and maybe ringlets to frame the face." She turned toward Trudy, "would that be too much trouble?" she asked.

"No Miss, it would be my pleasure. But we'll start with the roll, get you all pinned up and then I'll get the iron," Trudy said as she ran her fingers through Abigails long auburn locks. Within moments her hair had been twisted and rolled, pinned high on her head, "do you have adornments, a comb, feathers or a hat, Miss?" she asked as she turned and retrieved the heating iron, carefully twisting Abigail's hair round and round the rod, then releasing and watched as the auburn hair sprung free in a dancing ringlet, she did it again and again and once she'd finished, Abigail sat before the mirror, smiling up at the girl behind her.

"It's beautiful, Trudy. Thank you. I had thought to wear a bonnet, but maybe I should find some feathers as you suggest." She turned to Annabella, "is there anything you wish for me to assist with?" Her sister shook her head.

"No, you go, get dressed and return with your feathers. I intend to sit and be pampered," she said smiling at Trudy. "Mayhap I'll need your help dressing, Mama has only loaned me Trudy for a short time," she said rolling her eyes as Abigail laughed.

Back in her own room, with Molly following close behind, she moved toward her dress, ran her fingers over the slippery, cool satin, she loved the soft, silky feel against her skin. She turned away and began gathering her underthing's, moving behind the screen, she removed her housecoat and began to dress. Once she was ready, Molly took the gown from its hanger, and moved around the screen, holding it open for Abigail to step into. Once again, she enjoyed the sensation as satin smoothed up her legs, over her hips and higher to cover her breasts, her hands finding the armholes, she pushed her arms into the long, tightly fitting sleeves, the material settling snugly high on her upper arm, leaving her shoulders and neck bare. She pressed her palms to the front of her bodice as Molly threaded, pulled fastening the laces at her back. A belt created of the same material wound around her tiny waist causing the skirt to fall in a long flowing waterfall to the floor. Once finished, Abigail stepped around the screen to see herself in the long mirror, she looked lovely. The gown fitted like a glove, it was certain to attract Mr Langley's attention, especially as the bodice, pulled tight as it was, thrust her breasts up more than a little, her Mama would not be happy, but it was far too late to worry about that.

"You look stunning, Miss. Now, just slip your shoes on and we'll find those feathers. Maybe a little powder or charcoal," she studied the young woman before her and smiled, "No," she amended. "Perfect as you are."

"Thank you, Molly." She replied slipping her feet into the silver, low heeled shoes, admiring the embroidery. "These are quite pretty, I wonder where Ms Forester found them, they almost match my dress perfectly, I shall certainly have to thank her when next we meet."

Dressed, and with feathers in hand she traipsed back to Annabella's room with Molly in tow. Trudy opened the door on her way out, "You look lovely, Miss Abigail, here, I have but a moment," she moved behind her and situated the feathers, looked from the front and then removed them again, "I think you're perfect without them," she gave a quick curtsey and moved off up the hallway to her mistress's rooms.

Abigail and Molly assisted Annabella into her wedding dress, her sister holding tightly to her arm for balance as she stepped into the ivory silk pooling on the floor. Then with Abigail at the back and Molly at the front, they slowly slipped the material up, covering her under things. Annabella held out her hands as Abigail shimmied the bell-shaped sleeves up her arms and onto her shoulders, tucking, primping, and then holding her sister's long red hair whilst Molly concentrated on slipping the myriads of buttons through tiny buttonholes from collar to hip. Once completed, Annabella slipped on her shoes and stood as Molly adjusted her train, "well?" she asked.

"You are the most beautiful bride," Abigail said as she studied her sister from head to toe. The bodice was decorated with handmade crocheted lace and Ivory cord; and her trained skirt had the same lace sewn delicately along the long length of the hem. The bell sleeves held tight around her upper arm and from the elbow down hung loose and flowing, perfection. "Are you happy?" she asked, turning her sister to the mirror.

Annabella smiled, "Yes," she said after admiring herself for a few moments. "I'm ready, now we must wait for Mama to affix my veil. Meanwhile, Molly, could you possibly find some umbrella's," Abigail frowned, she hadn't heard any rain. She moved to look behind the curtain and watched as snow fluttered past the panes, "I don't relish the thought of going out in that, but an umbrella will at least keep us dry."

"Yes, Miss. I'll go and attend to that directly," Molly bobbed a curtsey and left.

"Here," Annabella said, holding a box out towards Abigail, "A small gift, I hope you like it."

Abigail opened the box and drew out a delicate, silver, filigree choker. "It's beautiful," Abigail crooned, "help me?" she held the lace out to her sister who took it and gently fitted it around Abigail's slender neck. It was the perfect finish to Abigails outfit. "I love it, thank you."

Abigail gently lifted the veil into her arms and turned to the door, "come on, let us go to Mama, and then we can find father to show him how well we look."

Their mother looked lovely in lilac, and she nodded her approval at Annabella's dress and frowned as she took in the open shoulders and the amount of exposed skin which Abigails dress failed to hide. She passed the veil to her mother, and Annabella bent dutifully as her mother slipped the comb into her red curls and draped the veil down over Annabella's face, the back, she fluffed up, and allowed it to drift and settle so it moved in tandem with the train when Annabella stepped forward.

The church was surprisingly warm, made so for the parishioners who'd dutifully paid their respects to God that morning. Both Annabella and Abigail sighed with relief; even after a short journey cramped together with their father and mama, the frigid chill had them shivering. The umbrellas lay discarded at the church doors, snow slowly melting and leaving tiny puddles. "It's time!" Mr Dumont stated as he snapped his pocket watch shut. Mrs Dumont patted Annabella's cheek softly and turned, then turned back.

"Abigail, Mr Langley is a gentleman, is he not?" Abigail looked at her mother in surprise and noted the wary look in her eye, and she realized her mother was worried, embarrassed even that Mr Langley may possibly divulge information. After all, her parents thought they'd been indebted to the man. Serves you right, Abigail thought, for sending me away to get my heart broken.

"Yes, Mama, of course."

Her mother moved then, swishing past the invited guests as they waited, acknowledging nobody until she reached the front pew where she inclined her head to Mr Ashcroft, who bowed in return, before settling herself onto the hard wooden pew.

Annabella clung to her father's forearm as she began the walk down the aisle, slow and graceful, her head held high, shoulders back, eyes finding those of Mr Ashcroft. Abigail followed, her eyes darting from one tall gentleman to the next and not finding the wide, muscular shoulders of Mr

Langley, her heart clenched and then clenched again as a gentleman to the right swirled to look as the bride drew closer to the pew where he stood, a face she would never forget; a face still mottled a slight purple from bruising, she dipped her head and prayed he would not recognize her. Mr Fletcher was at the wedding.

Trying to be as inconspicuous as possible whilst standing in front of the guests, Abigail was careful to keep her face turned away from where Mr Fletcher could see. How was she to dodge the man once the ceremony was concluded and with a dinner set for the guests? This beautiful moment was ruined for her. She missed the words spoken between Annabella and Mr Ashcroft, too inside her own head; only the raised voice of the vicar as he announced her sister and Mr Ashcroft as husband and wife, did she blink, pulled from her internal nightmare. Mr Ashcroft was raising Annabella's veil, and then Annabella was leaning toward her husband to accept his kiss. The ceremony was over. What was Abigail to do?

Chapter Forty

Ice crystals clung to Edwards lashes. His nose red, eyes watering, he was so bloody cold. He shivered as the snow piled higher on his hat, blanketing his shoulders and turning his dark coat, white. Time hadn't slowed as he had wished, and he was urging his mount to move as quickly as possible through the slippery, snow laden street, the church spiral in his line of sight, as he sagged in his saddle.

He was going to be too late! Exhausted, he slipped to the ground in front of the church, his legs nearly collapsing as he landed; the snow may be soft, but the cobbles below were hard, sending shock waves up his legs, and creating bolts of pain from knee to thigh, as he nearly stumbled. His focus was the door and as he swung it open, letting in the frigid air, he stood frozen, a snowman melting, the despair and anguish easily readable on his face. His heart fractured. He was too late. His hungry gaze travelled over Miss Dumont, now Mrs Ashcroft, taking in the fine dress, the curls which hung down her back, redder than he remembered, but then the light in the church was dim at best, especially to his snow burned vision.

She looked beautiful and she was kissing his cousin. He choked on a silent sob, and with a last lingering look, he turned his head, ready to leave and caught the gaze of non-other than Francis Fletcher, the man who had ruined him! If it hadn't been for his rumourmongering, Edward would have been seated beside his family, happy for his cousin, and a stranger to the auburn-haired beauty. He wouldn't have taken her, wouldn't have touched her, wouldn't have kissed and swallowed her moans of pleasure; he wouldn't have fallen in love.

"Get out," he bellowed pushing the door wide. Every face turned his way. He moved toward Francis with menacing intent in every line on his face. Francis stood his ground. From the moment the door had opened, letting the cold swirl around his feet, he had watched his former friend. Saw the anguish, the utter devastation wash across his face as he watched Spencer kiss his new bride, and he knew.

"Be very careful what you say, Edward," Francis warned. He moved toward Edward then, ready to meet him for a face down. The man had beaten him once, but now, Francis had the ammunition to tear this man's and his cousin's world apart.

"I warned you," Edward's voice was a growl, his hands fisted, but he held himself in check. After all, once Spencer learned that Francis was behind the rumour, his cousin would probably want first swing. "I made it brutally clear that if you EVER came near my family again, I would out you. Spencer," he cried, keeping a watchful eye on Francis, as he felt his cousin approach.

"I think we should take this outside, gentleman. Think of the ladies' susceptibilities, surely, they would not appreciate a brawl, in a church." Spencer's voice was low, but with his final words, a slight menace lingered.

Edward backed away, reversing his steps and the two well-dressed gentleman followed.

"What is this all about?" Spencer gritted out. "This is my wedding, how could you ruin it for me, after all I've been through."

"That's what I'm trying to tell you," Edward began, keeping his voice low, "It was Francis who started the rumour!"

Spencer stared at Edward for a moment and then turned his disbelieving gaze on the man who still wore the bruises from Edwards beating.

"At least I'm not the one tupping my cousin's fiancé." Francis's voice was not quiet, and gasps were heard echoing around the church. "Go on, ask him! He had Miss Dumont in Cornwall with him, I walked in on them kissing. Go on Edward, tell him," Francis almost hissed.

"Edward?" Spencer's eyes flew back to his cousin, who seemed to deflate before his eyes. They had everyone's attention now.

"I'm in love with Miss Dumont. I'm sorry, I n...' THWAK, the sound of skin hitting skin reverberated in the church and Edward took two stumbling steps backward, his hand to his face, his eyes burning with embarrassment and shame. For his cousin to call him out, had been his worst nightmare, but to do so in front of all his guests, humiliation burned. But Spencer was not done. He strode after Edward and another THWAK, sounded followed by yet another.

"Stop, stop it," he heard a woman's voice. "Mr Ashcroft, I beg you, please stop."

Spencer turned and eyed his wife who'd followed him down the aisle, "You weren't home when I called, you went away. You were with Edward?" he all but snarled. "Am I to be deceived at every turn. My wife, my cousin, my friend?"

"I, I," Annabella couldn't get her words out.

Edward was out the door now, his back hitting the snow-covered cobbles, he knew he should be inside defending Miss Dumont, but he was beat. He'd lost everything.

Chapter Forty-One

"Mr Ashcroft, stop, stop it," Abigail screamed as she fought her way through the guests filling the aisle, all of them vying for space to get the best view of the unprecedented proceedings. She pushed and shoved and finally came to stand beside her distraught sister.

"Annabella was at my aunts, Sir. It was I, that Mr Fletcher saw in Cornwall." She turned her angry face toward Mr Fletcher and the man turned white beneath his bruises. Oh yes, he knew he'd just made a huge mistake. She turned her face back to her new brother-in-law, "Mr Langley has done you no wrong, Sir, and you've done him an enormous disservice, after tracking down that bastard," all the ladies gasped into their handkerchiefs and the gentleman laughed behind their hands at the course language, and in a church no less. "Mr Langley discovered Mr Fletchers treachery and look at him, he still wears the colours where your cousin defended your honour. Now let me pass!"

She ignored the screams of the woman behind her, ignored the sounds of fighting as Mr Ashcroft launched his attack on Mr Fletcher. Her gaze was firmly fixated on the prone figure on the cobbles, the snow gently gathering on his face and clothes.

She didn't feel the cold wind, didn't acknowledge the snowflakes landing on her bare shoulders. Her skirt swirled around her legs as she moved to her beloved, and then the snow was melting beneath her knees, wetting her gown and dirtying the material. "I love you too, Mr Langley," she whispered. "Stay with me."

Chapter Forty-Two

Edward was dreaming. He had to be. Soft footfalls, the tiny squeak of shoes on snow and he prayed the steps belonged to Miss Dumont. He fought to open his eyes wider than the thin slits they were, but his vision blurred, from the beating, his exhaustion and the snow. Had she come to him? He tried in vain to make out the beautiful ivory skirts, but there was nothing, nothing except the swirling, silvery mist. He was back on the moor, the whirling mist rolling in around him, cold and unforgiving, his eyes closed.

His dream was not peaceful, there was noise, and movement. People yelling, yet he couldn't make out the words. So cold, so very cold, he was drifting. And then silence.

Sound came back, softly spoken whispers, the crackle of a fire, he was warm; had Jackson discovered his body? Was he no longer lost to the moor; he'd been so cold? His head moved side to side, and he fought to see, to open his eyes, and then he shivered violently as cold ate at his brow, feverish he drifted, his face was nothing but pain, his scar, had he been cut again? A nightmare. "Shh," a voice soothed, and a hand stroked his hair. His breath stuttered in his throat, and he calmed. Dreaming, dreaming, silence.

Movement woke Edward. He lay very still, waiting. His body heavy, his shoulder numb, and his fingertips tingled. His eyes felt puffy and tight and when he attempted to part his lids he succeeded only in squinting, eyes narrowed slits, up at the white ceiling. Where was he? He stiffened as he once again felt movement, something warm, silken brushed against his knee and then three things happened simultaneously. He bolted upright. Whatever had been pinning his shoulder was pitched forward, and the door swung open.

Jackson stood motionless in the doorway, for the briefest moment he just stared and then his face broke into a wide smile. "Ye really should start locking yer door, Sir," he said grinning at the startled pair in the bed. And then, as if there were no awkwardness at all in the situation queried, "Would ye like some tea?"

"Tea for two sounds lovely, thank you Jackson," Abigail responded. He gave a nod and shut the door.

Edward turned and his gaze clashed with sparkling, laughing green eyes. "What are you doing?" he croaked.

"Mr Langley, I recalled a tried-and-true technique, used when one is frozen and unconscious," she bit off her words and waved her hand indicating the two of them in the bed's close quarters. She raised her eyebrows and gave him a coy smile.

Edward raised the blanket, took a deep breath and quickly let it drop. "You're naked, Miss Dumont," he said incredulously.

"Yes, I didn't wish to wet the sheets, my gown was fair dripping from kneeling in the snow," she was enjoying herself tremendously, grinning at the traumatized look upon his face, and she wondered if that was what her own face had looked like when she'd woken with him naked beside her.

"But why, I mean what, oh no," he breathed, as he remembered. "The wedding, I interrupted the wedding!"

"Yes, indeed you did. And a spectacular interruption it was. Fists flying, men encouraging, while the women screamed. There were bloody noses, yours included tears and bruises. It was a very eventful day.”

“Spencer?” he asked, his face ached from his cousin’s fists, “Is he hurt?” He must be devastated, when the cousin he’d trusted had made a farce of the wedding, and now, to top it off, Miss Dumont was in his bed. There was no way that Spencer wasn’t hurt.

“Mr Ashcroft is perfectly fine. Some bruised knuckles, most of which I think he’s quite proud of,” she replied.

Edward touched his swollen nose; he deserved this and more. But to think Spencer was proud that he’d humiliated him hurt more than a broken nose.

Abigail pulled his hand away and entwined their fingers, “he’s not proud of that,” she said, “only that he laid out Mr Fletcher for the lies and hurt the man has inflicted on your family.” She pulled him down until he lay back on the pillows facing her. He edged away so their skin no longer touched, and she frowned. “Mr Langley, may I ask you something?”

“Certainly, and if it is within my power to answer, I shall do so.”

“Why do you pull away from me? You kiss me but then grow cold and distant. That night you touched me, and when I pleaded for more, you turned away. Just now, your body touched mine, yet you shied back. I don’t understand. Twice now, you have declared your love for me. How can you love me and not wish to touch me?”

“Miss Dumont,” he brought his hand up and gently pushed the hair from her face, his thumb softly wiping a fallen tear from her cheek. “I’ve loved you, almost from the moment I first saw you. I tried to restrain myself, but the temptation to touch you, to taste your lips was too great. I want you so badly that I ache, but each time I yield to my urges, to touch, to kiss; guilt rears its head, and I remember that you don't belong to me. I walked away every time, because if I'd stayed near you, my guilt may not have been enough to deter me from reaching for you again."

"I, oh," she breathed, "y-you mean the guilt of lying to me about my father and why you, for want of a better word, abducted me," she gave a small smile.

"Partly, but Spencer deserves …"

There was a quiet knock at the door and Abigail called "Enter."

There was a rattling of teacups, and the door swung open. "Jackson said you were awake Mr Langley, and I knew you'd be dying for a cup of tea, Abbey." Annabella said walking into the room with Spencer hot on her heels.

He stopped abruptly. "My apologies, Miss Dumont. I, err did not realize you were," the blush pinkened his cheeks as he spluttered. "Excuse me," and with a stiff bow, turned back to the door.

"Mr Ashcroft," Abigail called, "please, just give me a moment, I'm sure you wish to visit with your cousin. Annabella, my dress, if you'd be so kind." Annabella picked up the mud splattered gown.

"You can't wear this, Abbey. A moment," she held her finger up and walked swiftly from the room, her skirts swishing as she moved.

"Am I dreaming still," Edward asked. "My cousin is here?"

"Where else would he be, this is his home," she replied and before anything more could be said, Annabella returned and held up her housecoat. Abigail climbed from the bed, boldly staring at Mr Langley, his eyes ate her up as she slipped her arms into the long sleeves and pulled the belt tight about her waist. Edwards eyes darted back and forth between the two women. The stranger with her long red hair and green eyes, just as Spencer had described, and beside her, Miss Dumont with her auburn locks and deep green orbs; sisters. He hadn't known, Fletcher obviously hadn't known either as he'd called him out on his behaviour. He'd almost lost her for nothing. Hope flared deep in his chest. "Annabella, please call Mr Ashcroft back in," Abigail requested, "I'm sure he's eager to visit with his cousin." All eyes turned to the door.

Edward lay against the pillows. His head a mass of confusion at this new exciting discovery, his breathing uneven and his cock hard from the glimpse of Miss Dumont in all her glory, and suddenly there were two to many people in the bedroom.

"Edward," Spencer's voice rasped as he walked across the room, stopping beside Annabella. "I am in your debt,

Abigail stepped forward. "No, no debts," she interrupted and rolled her eyes at the man in the bed.

Edward smiled, or at least he attempted to with his split lip and broken nose. Then he turned to face Spencer, and eyed the couple before him, their hands clasped. His cousin looked down to where his gaze rested. "Ah, you've not yet officially met my wife, cousin. Edward, this beautiful woman is the light of my life, may I present Mrs Annabella Ashcroft, formerly Miss Dumont."

<u>**Epilogue**</u>

Abigail stretched languorously. She smiled as she felt the unfamiliar ache.

There had been no banns read, no elaborate wedding. As soon as Mr Langley was once again mobile, he'd not wasted a moment in seeking out a clergyman to purchase a common license and within days, Abigail had become Mrs Abigail Langley.

They were travelling back home to Cornwall, after a slightly tearful farewell with her sister and her new husband with promises of future visits, as they waved goodbye to the pair standing on the platform and watched as they grew smaller as the train puffed its way along the track.

Yes, Abigail had put her foot down. She refused to ride three days in hired boxes in such freezing temperatures, when they could arrive in Plymouth within six hours and collect their own much more comfortable carriage for the final leg of their journey. Mr Langley had grumbled but at his wife's insistence had resigned himself to the noisy monstrosity.

Plymouth would forever hold a place in Abigail's heart, after-all her innocence had been lost there, when Edward, unable to wait until they reached Cornwall, had succumbed and 'touched her' as she'd previously pleaded.

She rolled toward her husband, only now realizing he was awake and watching her as she stretched, straining the muscles along her arms and legs, her back lifting slightly from the mattress.

"I bet I could make you arch like that for me," he whispered, his lips close to her ear, making her shiver in delight.

"I'd wager the same!" she stated already reaching for him. He hissed as her hand wrapped around him.

"That's cheating, Mrs Langley," he said as his breath stuttered in his throat as her hand began to move.

"Yes, yes, it is," she whispered against his lips.

They both lost, or they both won, depending on one's interpretation.

Jackson closed the carriage door after Edward assisted his wife up the step, then climbed to the bench for the final leg. He clicked to the horses, their hooves danced, and the wheels rolled. They made good time, and when the sun broke through the clouds, sending shards of light to dance over the moor, Abigail eagerly leaned forward to stare out of the window, waiting with bated breath for the towering grey structure to come into view. The building she'd thought never to see again. The one she'd wished to become mistress off and now her wish had been granted. When it finally came into sight, she drank in its grandeur, then happily sank back into the cushions, cuddled warm and content within her husband's arms and sighed. "It's good to be home."

Alreet – from 'are you alright'. Not really used as a question, more as a greeting.
Bleddy – a Cornish way to say bloody

<u>Acknowledgements</u>

My darling husband for putting the book together and
creating the artwork for the cover.
And a huge thank you to my readers.